bad machinery

THE CASE OF
THE MODERN MEN

ONI PRESS

AN ONI PRESS PUBLICATION

bad machinery

THE CASE OF
THE MODERN MEN

by
John Allison

Edited by
Ari Yarwood

Designed by
**Hilary Thompson
& Sonja Synak**

PUBLISHED BY ONI PRESS INC.

founder & chief financial officer **Joe Nozemack**
publisher **James Lucas Jones**
editor in chief **Sarah Gaydos**
v.p. of creative & business development **Charlie Chu**
director of operations **Brad Rooks**
director of publicity **Melissa Meszaros**
director of sales **Margot Wood**
marketing design manager **Sandy Tanaka**
special projects manager **Amber O'Neill**
director of design & production **Troy Look**
senior graphic designer **Kate Z. Stone**
graphic designer **Sonja Synak**
digital prepress lead **Angie Knowles**
senior editor **Ari Yarwood**
senior editor **Robin Herrera**
associate editor **Desiree Wilson**
editorial assistant **Kate Light**
executive assistant **Michelle Nguyen**
logistics associate **Jung Lee**

onipress.com
facebook.com/onipress
twitter.com/onipress
onipress.tumblr.com
instagram.com/onipress

scarygoround.com

First Edition: July 2019

ISBN 978-1-62010-437-8
eISBN 978-1-62010-438-5

1 2 3 4 5 6 7 8 9 10

JACK

LOTTIE

SHAUNA

LINTON

SONNY

MILDRED

LITTLE CLAIRE

GRANDPA JOE

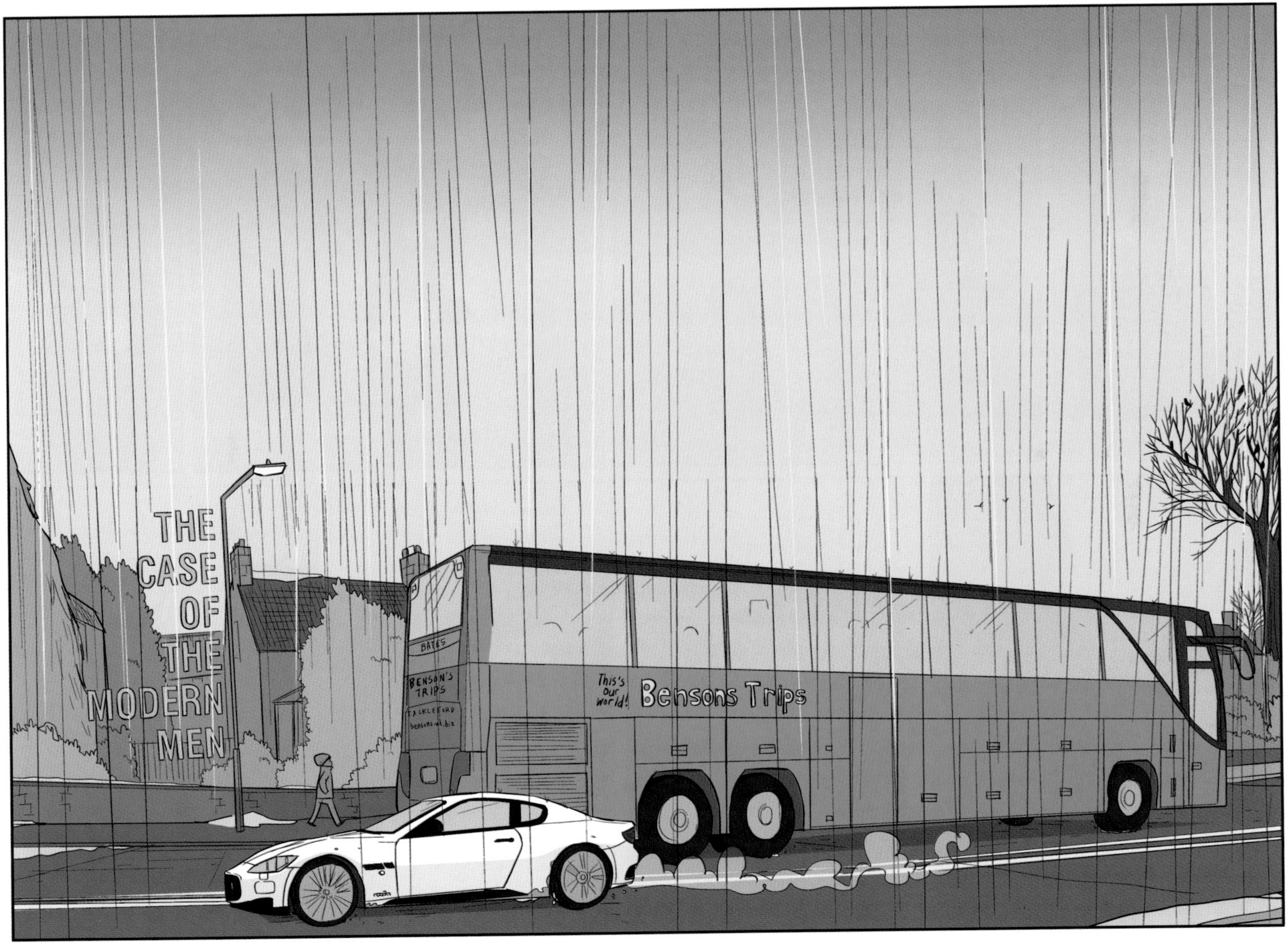
THE CASE OF THE MODERN MEN
BATES
BENSON'S TRIPS
TACKLEFORD
bensons-uk.biz
This's our world!
Bensons Trips

BUS IS HERE!

Lottie, what do you think they'll be like?

The French are well sophisticated, Little Claire.

Expect to emerge from this international meeting like a lovely new butterfly.

Cor. EXTHITING. Mine's called Camille. What's yours called?

Mimi. She seemed quite fun in her letters.

She likes music and photography! CULTURAL.

Hi, I'm Charlotte.

CLICK

FOR MY MEMORIES.

Ze weather, it is disgusting to me.

Yeah uh it rains a lot here, sorry.

My mum's waiting in the car.

Cars are destroying the planet.

Oh my God she is SUCH a *stroppy madam.*

REMAIN POLITE.

AVOID DIPLOMATIC INCIDENT.

Your car. It is... very GREEN.

Yes. See? My mum takes the environment very seriously.

Mum, this is Mimi Broussard.

Hello. You can call me Karen.

KAREN! Mum is trying to impress! Impress *France*!

Mum, can *I* start calling you Karen?

Of course Lottie. If you want to break my heart into a million pieces.

What about "Kaz"? Wait, or KAZZER?

Slow yourself down, Sonny. That stride of yours keeps getting longer.

Sorry Grandpa Joe.

You and your cousin are growing like weeds.

What do they feed you these days?

Er just basic food. Pheasant!

I didn't crack five foot until my 16th birthday.

I blame Capstan Full Strength and the national loaf.

You see these?

Milk teeth.

So what do you think? Could you fix it? It's only £90.

Ee, Sonny, I dunno. That's not a scooter, it's the memory of one.

Have you got the ninety nicker?

Nearly! I will have when I get my pocket money this weekend.

KLASSIC KORNER

E285   £90   E2

I can't ride one for two years, I just thought it might be something nice to do together.

Just so long as you don't mind me telling you wild tales of my youth. HEH!

Leave out the ones that end with a girl getting sent to Ireland.

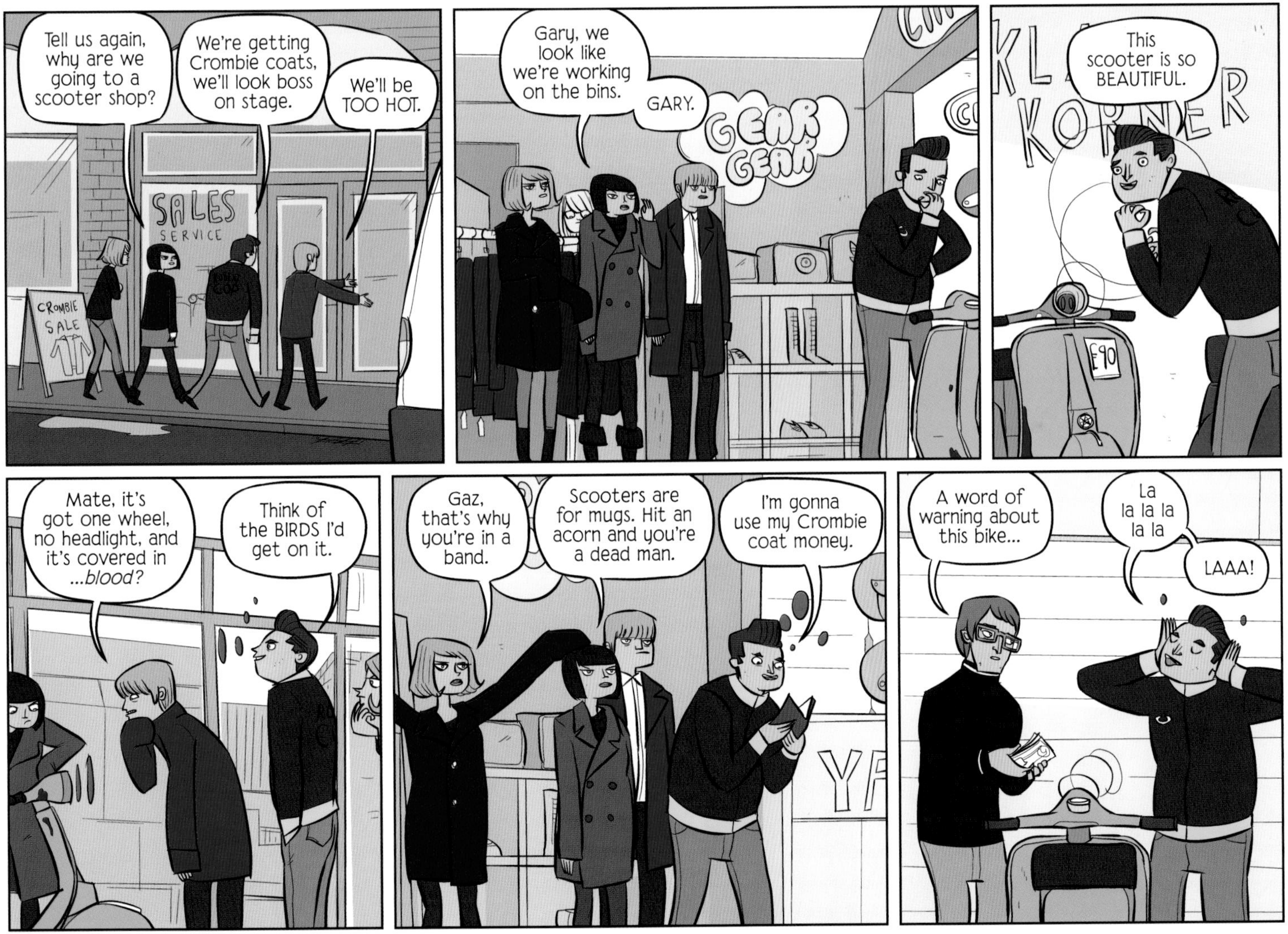
Tell us again, why are we going to a scooter shop?
We're getting Crombie coats, we'll look boss on stage.
We'll be TOO HOT.
SALES
SERVICE
CROMBIE SALE
Gary, we look like we're working on the bins.
GARY.
GEAR GEAR
This scooter is so BEAUTIFUL.
£90
Mate, it's got one wheel, no headlight, and it's covered in ...*blood?*
Think of the BIRDS I'd get on it.
Gaz, that's why you're in a band.
Scooters are for mugs. Hit an acorn and you're a dead man.
I'm gonna use my Crombie coat money.
A word of warning about this bike...
La la la la la la
LAAA!

Grandpa said he'd never seen a Vespa in worse condition and still intact, Jack!

That's... great?

What if it falls apart on our way home?

I've brought some carrier bags. And a dustpan and brush.

What if the wheels come off?

Couldn't your Dad have driven us back?

He says you appreciate something more if you've had to bear its dead weight five miles.

SALES
SERVICING
REPAIRS
TYRES
PARTS-
NEW
S/H

It's... gone!

Check inside, Sonny.

Excuse me, do you still have the 1963 Vespa 50? The £90 one?

Sorry mate, a lad bought it about an hour ago.

Arrrgh. I'll never find one like it again.

We get old bikes in all the time.

But nothing ever matches up to your first love.

Lighten up. You're driving away custom.

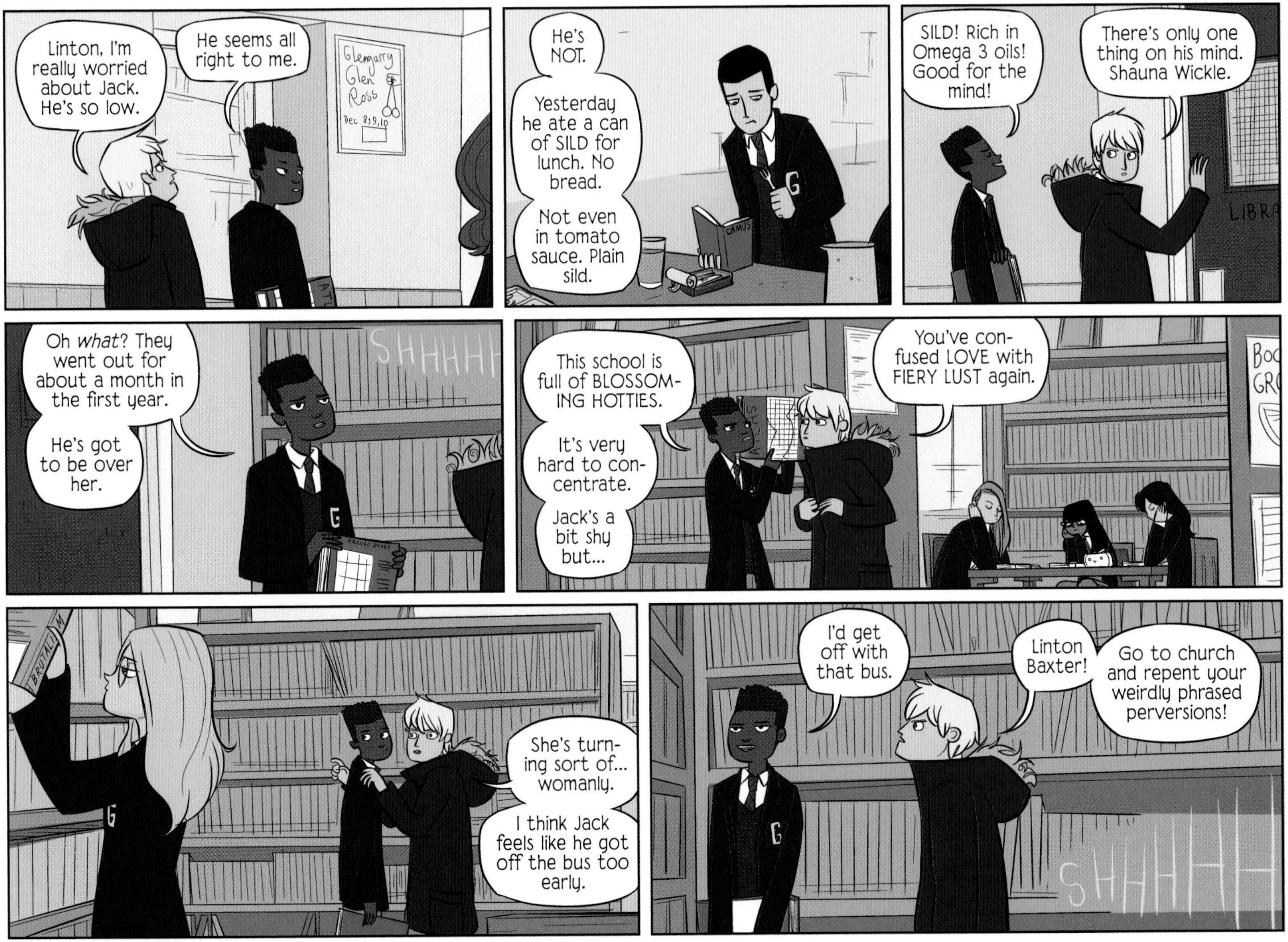
Linton, I'm really worried about Jack. He's so low.
He seems all right to me.
Glengarry Glen Ross Dec 8,9,10
He's NOT.
Yesterday he ate a can of SILD for lunch. No bread.
Not even in tomato sauce. Plain sild.
CAMUS
SILD! Rich in Omega 3 oils! Good for the mind!
There's only one thing on his mind. Shauna Wickle.
LIBRA
Oh *what*? They went out for about a month in the first year.
He's got to be over her.
SHHHHH
This school is full of BLOSSOMING HOTTIES.
It's very hard to concentrate.
Jack's a bit shy but...
You've confused LOVE with FIERY LUST again.
BRUTALISM
She's turning sort of... womanly.
I think Jack feels like he got off the bus too early.
I'd get off with that bus.
Linton Baxter!
Go to church and repent your weirdly phrased perversions!
SHHHHH

Bad Machinery, Volume Eight

Mum, Mimi is a ruddy nightmare.

Oh come on, Lottie, she's just in a strange place.

All I know is that if it was ME, I'd well be getting into it.

Not being all MARDY in my room.

You wouldn't be hiding in the kitchen with your mum?

I'm not HIDING.

I'm preparin' a KALEIDOSCOPE OF HOSPITALITY.

Laa! Brewing up for STAR NAMES!

Café pour... DEUX

Mimi what the FLIP are you doing?

You can't smoke in here! Mum will go mad!

HEY!

SUP

Augh.

My cigarettes are dead.

And now you kill coffee.

She emerges.

No doubt her breakfast demands will be *continentally elaborate*.

Help yourself to cereal, Mimi.

Did you sleep well?

Yes, thank you, Karen.

Ah mon dieu who is zis. You are so JOLI!

That's Pepper. I imagine he'll bite you.

Don't listen to her. He's sweet as anything.

Nooo, he loves me!

Ha ha!

A house... *of turncoats.*

Charlotte, zat coat.

It is like... ze coat for... ze hot water thing. No?

Excuse me? I love this coat!

I don't look like a hot water tank!

No no. Of course not, no.

PICK

Is more like... *Bibendum*? Ze Michelin Man.

Étrange! Per'aps you are related?

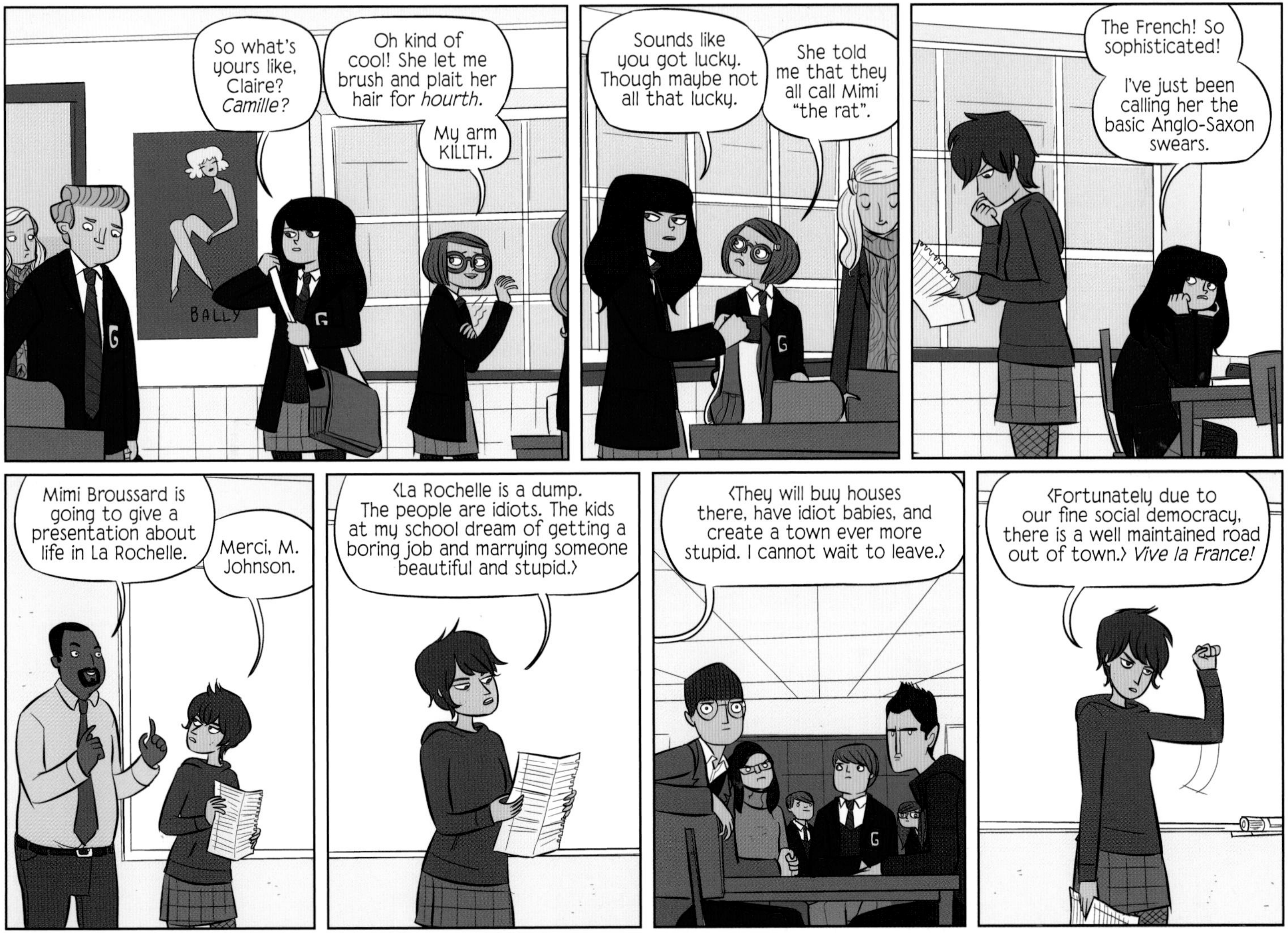

So what's yours like, Claire? *Camille?*
Oh kind of cool! She let me brush and plait her hair for *hourth.*
My arm KILLTH.
BALLY
Sounds like you got lucky. Though maybe not all that lucky.
She told me that they all call Mimi "the rat".
The French! So sophisticated!
I've just been calling her the basic Anglo-Saxon swears.
Mimi Broussard is going to give a presentation about life in La Rochelle.
Merci, M. Johnson.
‹La Rochelle is a dump. The people are idiots. The kids at my school dream of getting a boring job and marrying someone beautiful and stupid.›
‹They will buy houses there, have idiot babies, and create a town ever more stupid. I cannot wait to leave.›
‹Fortunately due to our fine social democracy, there is a well maintained road out of town.› *Vive la France!*

<Oh bravo, Rat. Bravo.>

FRAPPE FRAPPE FRAPPE FRAPPE

Sonny, why aren't you on the French exchange?

I thought your family loved France? Don't you have a house there?

It's more of a cottage.

Dad says we've put enough money into the French economy.

He's not willing to...

...feed and shelter some spotty youth, just so you can go and live on Nutella for a fortnight.

Your Dad's funny.

He's sort of funny. In a way.

Hey, English boys?

Do you two have a cigarette? I am going insane.

Um er no sorry bye.

CRUMPLE

So SMOOTH.

I think it was the "bye" that really dazzled her.

CLAP

You know who smokes? Jack's sister and her mates.

I'm very intimidated by Jessica, Linton. She's deputy head girl.

It's pronounced "aroused", Son.

SHUT UP!

Jack, can you crash a cig off your sister?

It's a matter of life and death.

Smoking won't make you seem cool, Linton.

You've got the flat top now. All you can do is wait and see if it takes.

SNAP

Please Jack, PLEASE! That French lass wanted a cigarette.

Which one?

The one with the... big crest of hair.

I can probably nick one off Jess at home.

No! We need it now!

She'll be in the sixth form common room. He can't go in there.

The only obstacles... *are in your mind.*

Saying something in a mysterious way DOESN'T MAKE IT TRUE.

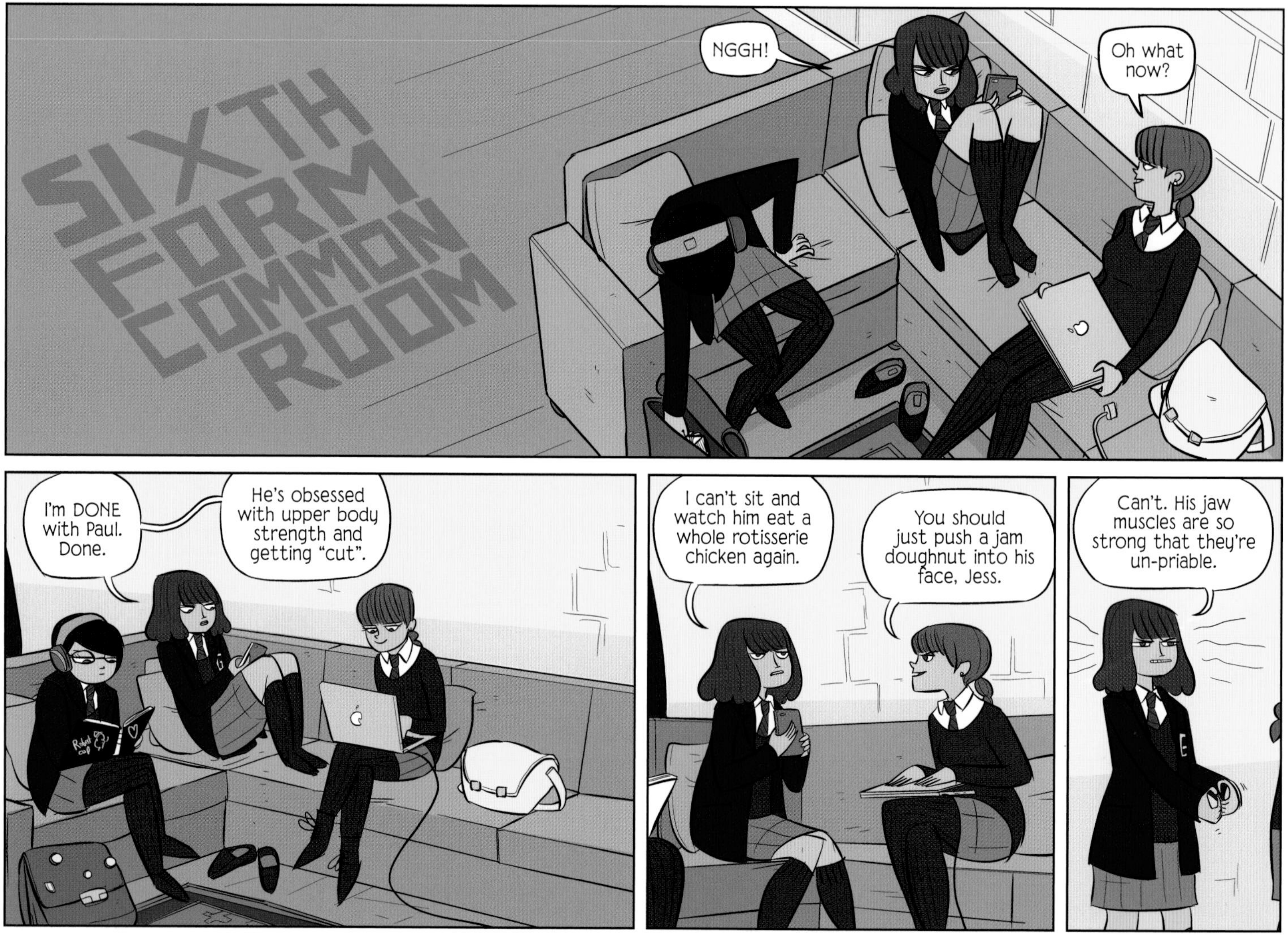
SIXTH FORM COMMON ROOM
NGGH!
Oh what now?
I'm DONE with Paul. Done.
He's obsessed with upper body strength and getting "cut".
I can't sit and watch him eat a whole rotisserie chicken again.
You should just push a jam doughnut into his face, Jess.
Can't. His jaw muscles are so strong that they're un-priable.

All you've got to do is go in there, ask your sister for a cig, and go.

The entire process will take two minutes.

If you take out the time spent walking, it's probably 20 seconds tops.

NOTHING.

Why should I risk humiliation just so you can impress a girl I've not met?

Liam Salkeld lost his trousers in the common room, Linton.

And he'd been sent in to tell someone their DAD HAD DIED.

Looking in there, Jack. I see what you mean.

SHOVE

6TH FORM COMMON ROOM

SLAM

What you just did was HORRIBLE.

The greatest warriors are forged in the hottest fire.

Conan... didn't even *wear* trousers.

RATTLE

Isn't that your little brother?

Oh EFF EFF ESS.

Jack, you have to get out of here immediately.

Let him stay!

Um I just wanted to know if I could have a cigarette.

I don't smoke!

That's partially true.

She doesn't smoke when she's *asleep*.

Oh, give him a ciggie, you beast.

I'm not going to start my own brother smoking.

Cigarettes are a terrible vice. We're all giving up.

They just help with exam pressure.

We were lured in by those collector's cards of rotten mouths, bad lungs and gangrene.

The tobacco industry is a very finely tuned marketing machine.

It's not FOR me! It's for a girl!

AWWW!!

No! It's for someone else! I don't even want to impress her!

AWWW!! *Denial is the first sign!!*

Have three. Space 'em out. That'll get you there.

But you have to promise to tell us EVERYTHING.

BUT

At its bitter core, even victory is sour.

MUSS   RUFFLE

Good luck, Jack, and I'm head girl, so remember, if you chicken out, I'll give you detention.

Heh okay, thanks Lauren heh *heh*

Oh wow, you have a NEGA ZAXXON machine! The first ever game to feature power-ups!

It was a huge flop. Most of the motherboards had to be buried in the desert.

People weren't ready for it yet.

Sometimes being too early is as bad as being too late.

ENEMY JERKS *20

FUEL E

I got them! I got them! I got the-

Yes?

-sixth-formers' opinions on *sensible GCSE options.*

As you were, boys.

Bell just went, Jack. We missed our French girl window.

But Linton and I have been talking and we want you to know that we respect you *a lot.*

You're sure Mimi is Lottie's exchange partner?

Wishing won't change it, Linton.

I find Charlotte very... hard to talk to.

Well, her mind moves a lot faster than ours.

Er, speak for yourself.

I went on the internet, *got it made official.*

RUMMAGE

Linton, Mensa's logo isn't in Comic Sans.

"Genius" has an "i" in it.

WELL what are you three doing on my door-step dressed for a wedding or perhaps... *funeral*?

We were wondering if Mimi was in.

She's filling her pen. Could take a while. The stationer recommended a full flush of the reservoir.

There are some boys outside. They seem keen to disappoint you.

I will put on my shoes.

Oh I feel REAL at last.

Well con-grats. You got Mimi smoking again.

She could have been a professional athlete.

Now, just another lousy street punk.

FLIC

Can we do something fun now? Where cool people are?

I am so bored.

We could—

We can't pretend to read foreign newspapers, Jack.

She'll know.

Why don't you take her under the bridge? The mods' nest!

Oh yes? Like... ze Sixties?

Imagine. Smartly dressed young men crazy for SCOOTERS! The WHOM &c.

Lottie, we're... too um... busy... to go under the bridge.

And by busy I mean scared.

We talked about going.

And we're going to look pathetic if we don't take her.

It'll take a hell of a waitress to get looking pathetic off the table, lads.

HUDDLE

HUDDLE

So what goes on under zis bridge?

Well er people compare scooters...

...and if you've not got a scooter, you just have to look your best.

Yeah, basically you pitch up in a blue plastic belted trenchcoat...

...and everybody goes "oooh".

NO. Mod is a LIFESTYLE.

It's about *clean living under difficult circumstances.*

CLEARANCE·4M

Who are these kids?

Most of them are from Wendlefield Academy.

Is that a ...*Vespa?*

No, it's a Tamoretti. It's a cheap and nasty Chinese knock-off.

What did you say?

TUG

And, may I add, a beautifully maintained example.

Lad here was knocking my ride.

N-no, sorry, I didn't mean it, I er

Ay ay ay what's going on.

That kid must be the local ACE FACE, the KING MOD.

Look at his HAIR

It's really tragic that you two have found love at the PRECISE SECOND YOU'RE GOING TO DIE.

It's not getting it to look like that, it's getting it to *stay* like that.

Calm yourself down, Pete. He's said sorry.

You three, clear off until you've learned some basic manners or until you start shaving.

Whichever comes later.

Girls, you can stay if you like.

No thanks, we... uh... we...

Lottie, you do not 'ave to make excuses to a man whose great romance is with 'is *comb*.

Oh, there's Shauna! Come on Mimi. You'll like her.

I will wait 'ere.

Please yourself.

That is what I am doing.

Jesus WEPT.

Well that could have been more embarrassing, I suppose.

I guess. We could have been naked. Or sung a song *a capella*.

Lottie, I've not seen you for days.

Oh GAW it is because of ruddy Mimi.

Is she a handful?

Imagine that I have a watermelon in each hand,

How are things with you, anyway? How goes THE PLAN?

Oh, well, well! In fact I really have to go now.

Bye Shauna!

Imagine that I've crushed both watermelons due to frustrating lack of facts in that update!

All right girls, I'll come and get you at 10.

We'll be here, Chief.

Lore, come on Mimi. I know you don't wanna do any of this but it's been *organised*.

At least *try* to have fun, maybe?

It's a bowling alley, not a funeral.

And bowling pins sort of... get resurrected over and over again.

Zey are trapped and doomed to repeat their mistakes.

What were you all laughing at, Camille?

Oh nothing, Claire.

Merci.

Mimi bowls like she wants to kill the skittles.

You're allowed to do a dance if you get a strike.

I am dancing... *inside*.

Hey RAT.

SIGH

<You have something in your hair.>

<No I don't.>

<Yes you do.>

SPUB

Did you jutht put chewing gum in her hair?

No. It was bubble gum.

Oh that'th DITHGUTHTING.

I'm sorry, Claire, my English is not so good.

I am really getting none of zis. *En français?*

MY LITHP GETTH WORTH WHEN I AM ANGRY, CAMILLE.

Come on, come with me.

I've never seen you like this!

It's just like real white hot rage... but cuter?

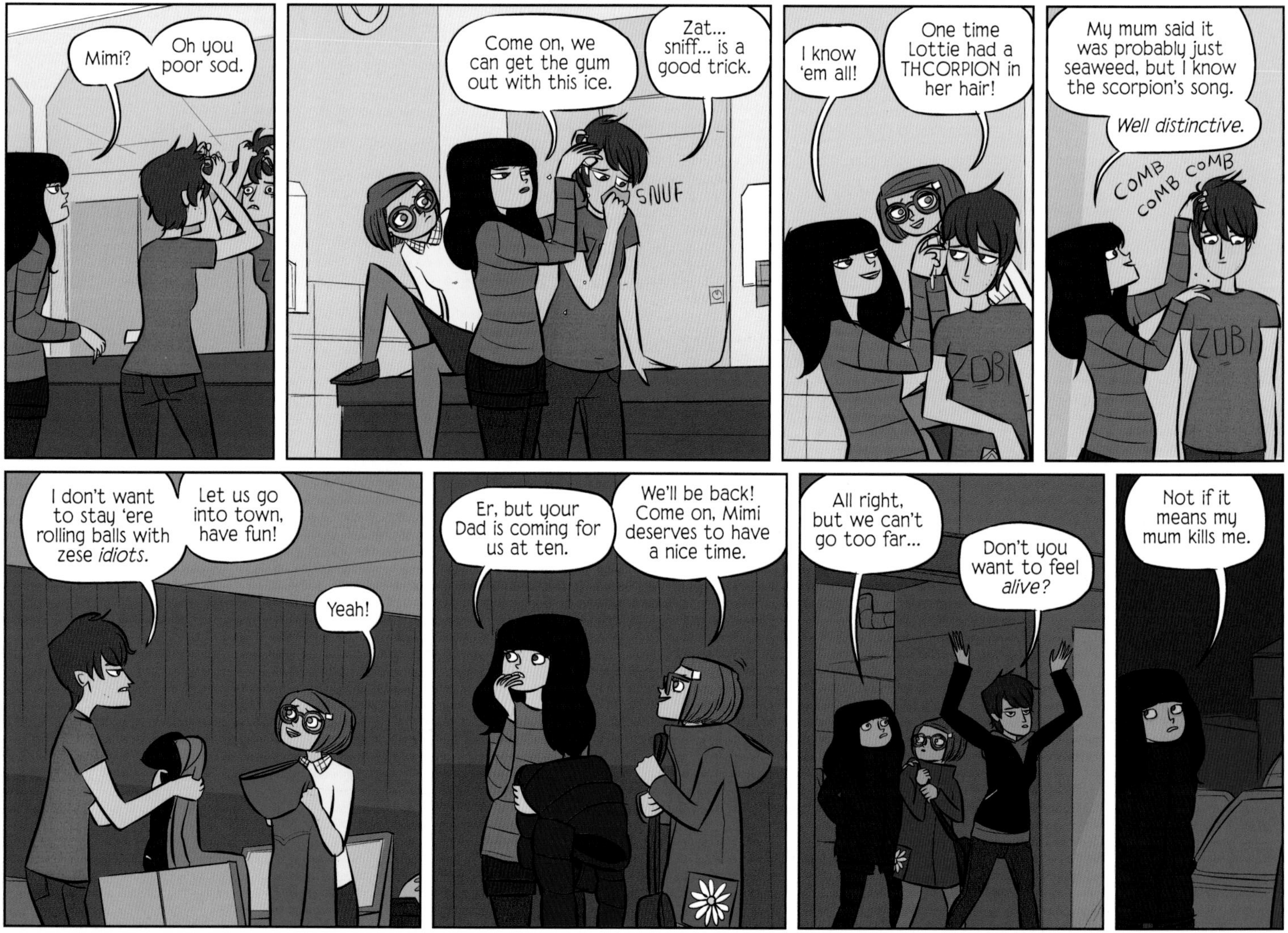
Mimi?
Oh you poor sod.
Come on, we can get the gum out with this ice.
Zat... sniff... is a good trick.
SNUF
I know 'em all!
One time Lottie had a THCORPION in her hair!
My mum said it was probably just seaweed, but I know the scorpion's song.
Well distinctive.
COMB COMB COMB
I don't want to stay 'ere rolling balls with zese *idiots*.
Let us go into town, have fun!
Yeah!
Er, but your Dad is coming for us at ten.
We'll be back! Come on, Mimi deserves to have a nice time.
All right, but we can't go too far...
Don't you want to feel *alive?*
Not if it means my mum kills me.
ZOBI

Leather jacket, maybe.

Puffer jacket, come back in a year or so.

As for her, you can't bring your babysitting to a bar.

Sorry girls. You've got to clear off. McDonalds is still open.

We do not want CORPORATE BEEF, you FASCIST!

Come on now, Mimi, the fascist is just doin' his job.

And don't get mad, Claire, your beautiful complexion is a gift 4 life.

SHOVE

There's no doorman on thith pub. And there'th a band playing!

"The Cod-Reggae All-Stars." What's *Cod Reggae?*

A type of music zat is preferable to standing in ze *freezing street?*

We can probably get away with going in if we don't try to buy booze.

But Claire might give us away.

Just walk in like you are meant to be zere. No one will ask a question.

I'm Claire Little and I DESERVE that island sound.

Are these the Cod-Reggae All-Stars?

Er no... I think this ith the thupport act.

Oh WHAT we're not even going to get to see the All-Stars.

DOORS 7:30

8·15 THE LITE FUNK EXPRESS

9.00 JIMMY BLUE JEANS

9·50 COD-REGGAE ALL-STARS

CURFEW

Mimi where did you get that WINE?

I found it. No one was drinking it any more.

Ugh! I would say that you don't know where that glass has been...

...but looking around, you do, and you made your decision.

This one is going out to the funk disciples dancing down the front.

From my thumb, to your feet, ladies.

I THINK... THE MUSIC... HAS GOT INTO MY *SOUL*!

LAAAA!!

Bwaaahhh!!!

Run run run we've got one minute to meet your dad!

He's just pulling in! There's Camille!

Did you have a nice time, girls?

YEAH!

CHEW

It was...all right.

Are you all right there in the front, Camille?

Hmm?

SPUB

TAP TAP TAP TAP TAP TAP

VRRRR

Oh no Claire now you are stuck with this monster.

IRE

Uh her her her her

Claire, I'm so sorry, I 'ave behaved so badly.

Maybe we can... get the gum out?

I cut it out. It will remind me... of my crime.

Sank you for showing me zat I 'ad gone too far. Good-night.

WHY DO I FEEL SO COLD?

Camille, would you like something to drink?

A glass of salt water will be all.

If you wish to spit in it, I will understand.

Ha ha ha haha! oh mon DIEU!

We did some total street justice on Camille.

Are the other kids that bad to you all the time?

It was much worse. Now I am defeated. I am ignored.

I count the days until I am 16.

Then, PFF, I am gone from school, goodbye.

Bon anni-versaire!

That is so UNFAIR!

She is a MONSTER. A MONSTER.

But we GOT HER.

THUMP THUMP

Lottie, she is like ze *dandelion*.

You think she is dead, but no.

Mimi, do you want to be friends?

I would like zat very much.

Do you want a hug?

No.

You and Camille weren't always enemies, were you?

I bet you were BESTIES, BFFs!

'Ow do you guess this? You are a *witch*.

Camille Duplass was my best friend when I was 8 years old.

We are, you know, *inséparable*?

We tell each other everything, every secret.

Then one day, a great revelation. She 'as six..? *Mamelons*?

Buttons?

Nipples. She is like a cat.

Mary and Joseph!!

And so this got out somehow?

Yes. She is destroyed. Years of torture.

A person... is changed by this. She leaves ze school.

At 11, we start ze same collége.

She blames me. And she is beautiful now.

She lies, she whispers, now I am made into a nobody. A RAT.

How many people did you tell about her... problem?

Everyone I told promised not to tell.

PRANG

VRAMM

SKID

Are you all right?

Yeah, just hit some ice, lucky I wasn't going fast.

Ohh look at it, oh noooo nooo.

My Grandpa can probably fix it! He can fix anything!

It's Paul, isn't it?

Yeah... wait, *I know you*, your mate was knocking my bike yesterday.

Sorry. Linton's not the most tactful person I know.

He's the least tactful person I know.

Heh! What a mess!

They're great, these Chinese bikes, until you finally decide to ride them.

Can you fix it?

Mods, coming around again! Takes me back to my days working at the Kaufman in '61.

I'd been a teddy boy, most teds hated mods. But I didn't care.

The girls! Pointy bras, hair lacquered just right, paradise for a lad.

The lads were purists and snobs, but at least they had manners.

We'd have all the villains in there too.

The Wessex Brothers.

Bonnie Prince Gordon.

Tony Crow and his mother!

Never any trouble, or if there was, it took place out the back.

They all just loved jazz, see?

But *can* you fix it?

Grandpa's in his *anecdotage*. Stories only stop for toilet breaks.

So Paul said we could go under the bridge whenever we wanted?

Yes! He said there'd be no trouble now.

Grandpa Joe did a really good job fixing his scooter.

Now we're here, what do we do? I feel weird.

POP

I don't like being under pressure to ENJOY MYSELF.

Omigod that's him, S-R-Sly?

We 'eard you saved Paul from the burnin' wreck of 'is bike!

That's absolutely not what happened.

So MODEST! So CUTE.

So... Jack... The Outsider. What's, er, it about?

It's about a man who is punished for not acting like everyone expects him to.

MIZZI

CAMUS The Outsider

Does it get shooty?

Briefly.

CAMUS The Outsider

This is incredible. There's a lad over there with 24 mirrors on his bike.

They're almost certainly a threat to his safety.

Sonny, that crest is... *wow.*

Those girls teased it up. I FEEL POWERFUL

What's going on?

The king of the mods is coming!

WHOA, and that must be the QUEEN!

Take of the helmet, take off the helmet...

OH

NO

LAUREN

Jack, if it's any consolation, you never had any chance with her, ever.

This just scientifically proves it.

Jack, are you all right? You look like you're going to be sick.

It's just... it's just... er...
OH WHAT'S THE POINT

Is Lauren your first love?

I mean, she's been your sister's best friend almost your whole life.

And you were... already sad... that she's leaving school this summer?

UH, NO.

Maybe.

We thought you were sad about Shauna, but this...

Stop comparing make-up tips, girls, something's going on.

Someone's challenged the king of the mods to his title.

How does this WORK?

What will CHANGE?

Just let it wash over you like the ocean, Linton.

Get your phone out and BING IT!

Who's challenging Sean to be king of the mods?

He's got a nice set of wheels though.

And his own mod coterie...

...two gimlet-eyed stunners...

I've never seen him before.

Me neither.

...and a lad picking his teeth clean with a stiletto knife.

PICK

Oh! He's got the bike I wanted to buy!

He's made a lovely job of it.

He got your bike?

Sonny, can't you *try* to be *unreasonable* about this fact?

WINCE

You're making him uncomfortable, Linton.

What's your challenge, challenger?

The Davy Jones.

Accepted. I've never heard of it though, mate.

Padre?

FLIP

TACKLEFORD-WENDLEFIELD CHAPTER

No one's called a Davy Jones since... 1983?

It's outlawed in most chapters.

But not this one.

The local Davy Jones involves a head-on chicken run down the canal towpath at Swafford Mill.

But there's only room to swerve one way down there...

...into the canal.

This isn't what mod culture is about.

It's *bloody ridiculous.*

I will watch, but only to frown throughout.

Sean, this is an incredibly stupid thing to do.

The crown's heavy, babe. Takes broad shoulders.

You know you're not... *an actual king?*

Tell that to them.

SEAN!

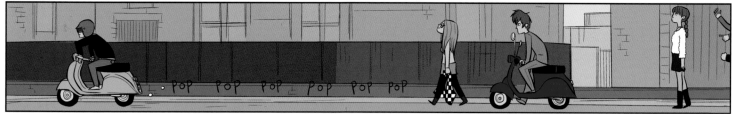

POP POP POP POP POP POP

46

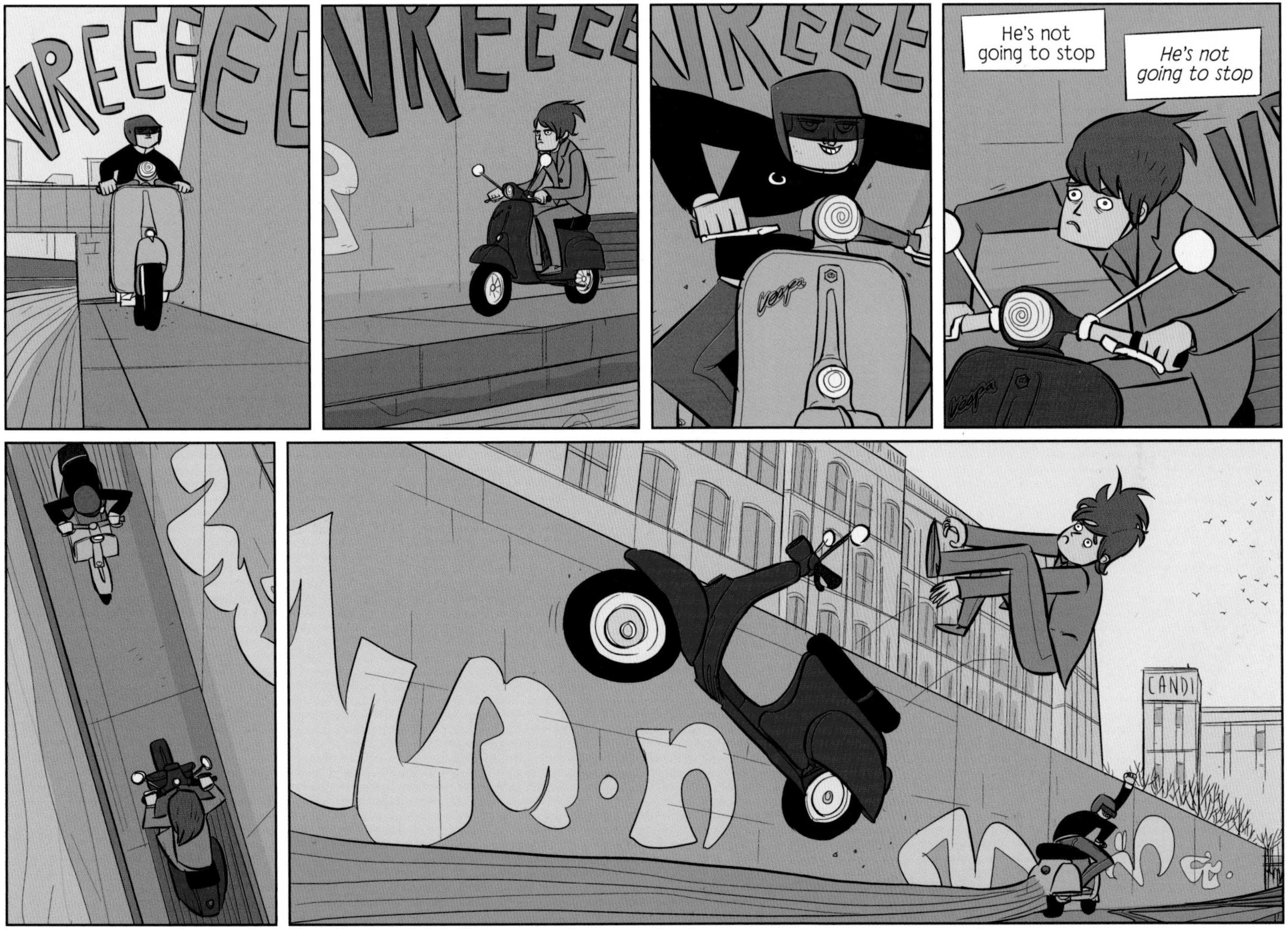
He's not going to stop
He's not going to stop
CANDI

GLOOP

In accordance with chapter law, the old king will be shorn of his crest.

SLICE

Hail the new king of the mods, er...

Gary Thickett

GARY THICKETT!

Come on lads, this is too weird.

It leaves a bad taste in your mouth.

...and they pretty much amount to shouting "Gary" with local barbarians.

I've got my limits...

Call me old fashioned.

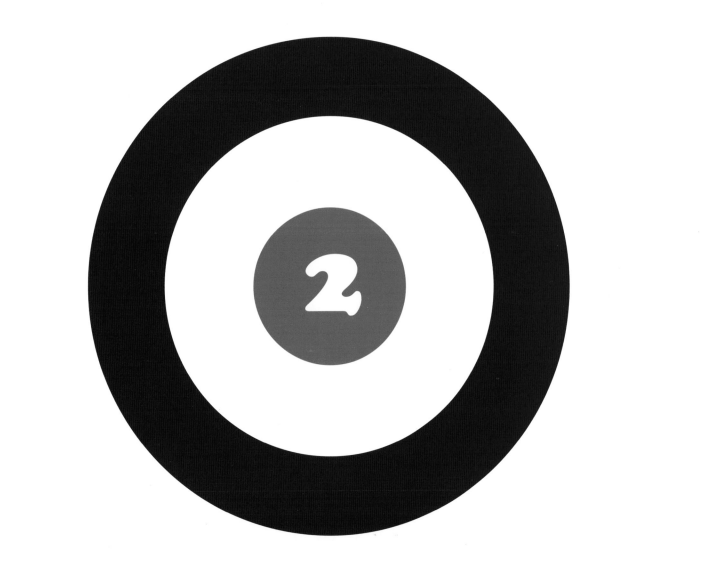

Six of 'em, Jack. She had six of 'em. Like a *cat*.

Had?

Four were surgically whipped off and she keeps them in a matchbox.

For her memories.

SNIP

This sounds like Lottie's trademark nonsense to me.

Cooked up in a brain permanently running at the legal limit.

LA!

SKIP

DO NOT TAKE HOT DRINKS OUT OF TUCK

CLUBS

Gary Thickett... Gary Thickett...

Are you sure he goes to our school?

He's in the book. 5th year.

There he is. Completely unremarkable.

Standard brownhair.

How does a lad like that become king of the mods in an afternoon?

Mods mods MODS!

You've all gone BARMY.

You don't understand modernism AT ALL.

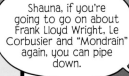

Shauna, if you're going to go on about Frank Lloyd Wright, Le Corbusier and "Mondrain" again, you can pipe down.

I went on Spotify and listened to them and they were all *rubbish*.

You got me, Baxter. You got me.

Hah!

POINT

POINT

HAH!

Linton, you are such a *wally*.

Steady, Jack!

Just had to upbraid another popinjay.

What is going *on?*

School is no time for flamboyant self-expression.

This "modern-ism" must be nipped in the bud.

At least they're dressed smart, Mr Knott.

Do you know what's smart, Mrs Lord?

CONFORMITY.

YOU BOY! That jacket is a BUM FREEZER! Un-hem it immediately!

SNIP!

YOU GIRL! You're wearing more makeup than Coco the Clown! Wash it off!

I have NO IDEA what to say about that waistcoat and pocket watch...

...but I'm giving you detention anyway!

SNIP!

That's her? Camille?

Yeah. I'm throwing shade in her general direction.

It looks like you've beaten her already.

She's a bully, Shauna. A tyrant. A no-good.

Oh Lottie, no...

I just want her to know I've still got my eye on her.

Hm.

France has given us fine cheese, the best wine, HOTE CO-TOOR and Marie Curie.

Pardon?

But of course, for every YANG there is a YIN.

For every DOVE, a CROW.

We need to stop 'er doing zis.

We must stop 'er NOW.

Lottie, come with US.

I just want you to know, this victory dance had the potential to be a LOT LONGER.

‹Two cheese-burgers with the gherkin discs removed.›

Merci, Hélène.

‹So. We have two weeks to destroy "Charlotte Grote".›

‹How do we go about this?›

SNARF SNARF

‹It will be hard.›

‹She seems to be popular through being pleasant and likeable.›

‹SHE IS A FAT ENGLISH COW!›

CLOP

‹I think it is just her coat that makes her look like that.›

‹Even by international standards she is beautiful.›

‹Such FLAIR!›

‹ARE YOU›

‹DISAGREEING›

‹WITH›

‹ME?›

‹By the time we leave, she will be nothing. Nobody.›

‹Now destroy your international beauty standards handbooks.›

‹We no longer recognise them.›

Hey FINCH

OH GOD

Sigh.

If you're going to call me Mr Spock...

...I just want you to know that I'm not going to renounce logic.

It's very useful.

Calm down mate, we just want to know where you get your hair cut.

Danny tried to get a Caesar at Half Cutz on Belmont Street, but they made him look like a monk.

It's not... *that bad*.

Pull the other one.

Well, er, I...

Don't be modest, Jack!

His dad cuts it! Jack's dad is a hairdresser! He's ace!

They respected me, Mildred. For one sweet minute they respected me.

If it's any consolation, Jack, I don't think they respected you all that much.

x

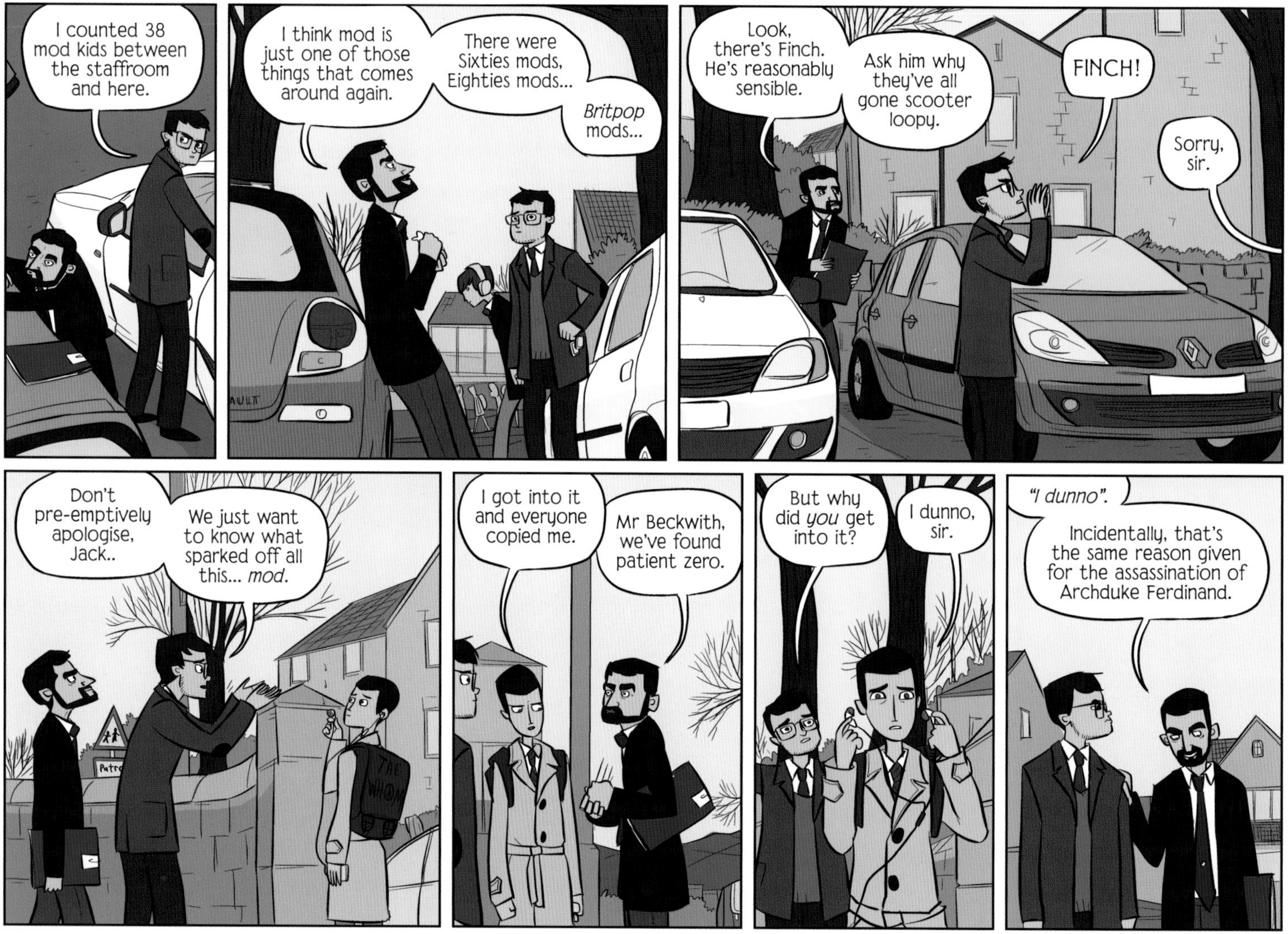
I counted 38 mod kids between the staffroom and here.
I think mod is just one of those things that comes around again.
There were Sixties mods, Eighties mods...
Britpop mods...
Look, there's Finch. He's reasonably sensible.
Ask him why they've all gone scooter loopy.
FINCH!
Sorry, sir.
Don't pre-emptively apologise, Jack..
We just want to know what sparked off all this... *mod.*
THE WHO
I got into it and everyone copied me.
Mr Beckwith, we've found patient zero.
But why did *you* get into it?
I dunno, sir.
"I dunno".
Incidentally, that's the same reason given for the assassination of Archduke Ferdinand.

VRURCH

So, BURY ME, IN SULPHUR, ATOMIC NUMBER 16, BOILING POINT 717.8 KELVINNNNN

We've been Brutalism UK! Good... AFTERNOON!

Holy Rosicrucian Order, Shauna!

Bravo bravo! MAGNIFIQUE!

CLAP

CLAP

How did you end up in a *power violence band* called "Brutalism UK"?

Well, I kept arguing with MODS who didn't understand MODERNISM...

...then I saw a poster...

Oh WICKED! At last, people who will under-stand me.

TUBA SQUAD

BRUTALISM UK

They turned out *not* to be a group celebrating mid 20th-century concrete architecture..

You have no idea how much I respect that you just went with it.

No idea.

Iggy and Rod say they're going down the rec. Do you two want to come?

Flip, I'd love to.

Mainly so I can find out what drives a lad called ROD.

But mum is making macaroons.

WHAT

Yeah I know. It never happened before.

It's all to impress Mimi, but I'm gonna enjoy this golden age while it ruddy lasts.

Ze Jaguar. Nice guitar.

You play ze drop-D tuning, yes?

CLICK

Yeah.

Cool.

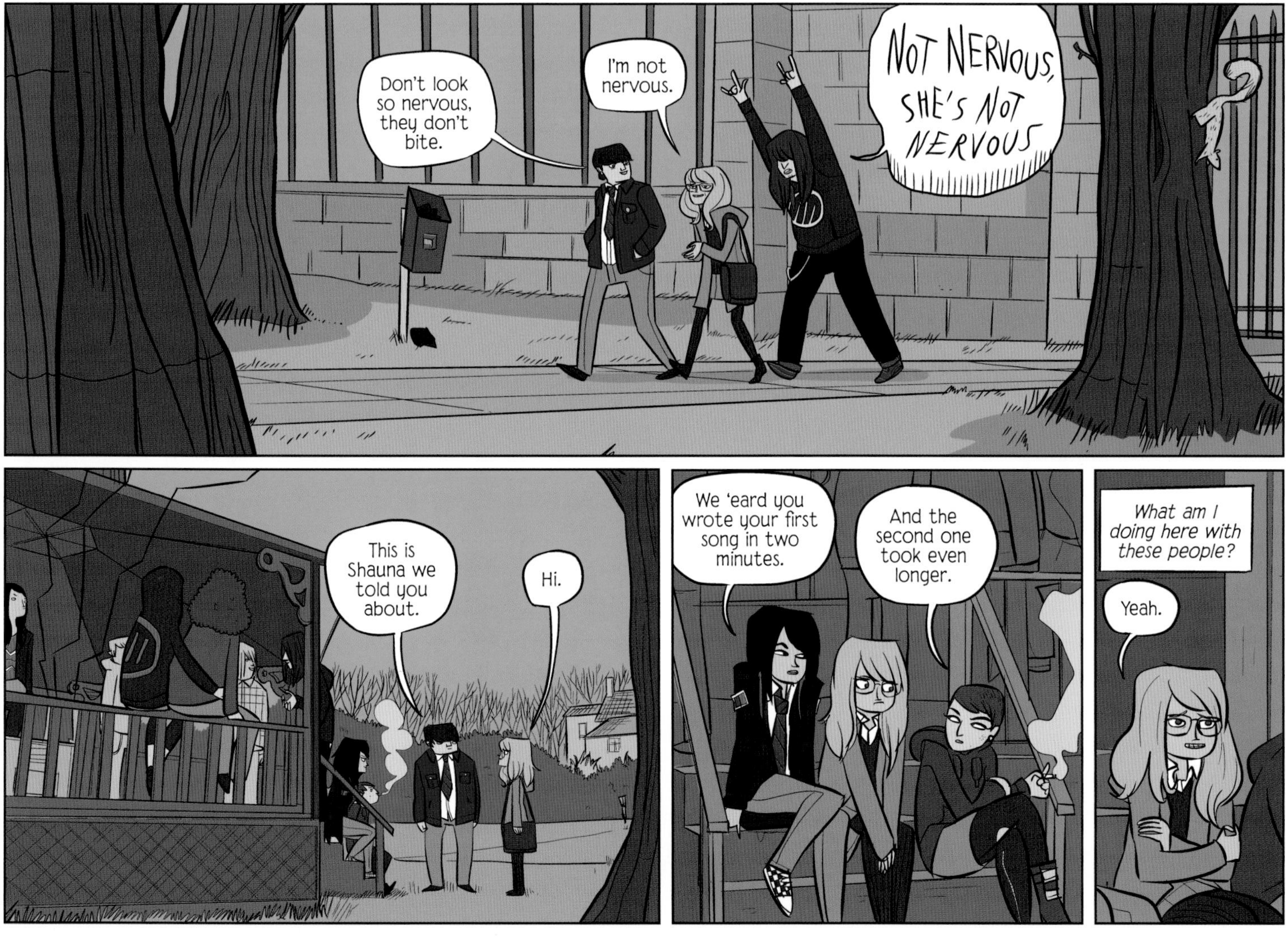
Don't look so nervous, they don't bite.
I'm not nervous.
NOT NERVOUS, SHE'S NOT NERVOUS
This is Shauna we told you about.
Hi.
We 'eard you wrote your first song in two minutes.
And the second one took even longer.
What am I doing here with these people?
Yeah.

Is it just ME or are those scooters following us?

Well. It is possible zey are travelling in ze exact same direction as us, at ze exact same speed.

Mimi, it's also possible that *my dog's bum smells like roses.*

I reckon one theory's about as likely as the other.

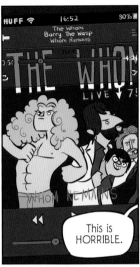

This is HORRIBLE.

Well, you're not meant to listen to The Whom on a phone speaker.

These are heavy songs, to be heard in quadrophonic sound. *Four speakers.*

Oh. Does the good music come out of the other three speakers?

Or does quadrophonic technology contain an algorithim...

...that converts the notes and words into better ones?

Best band, boys.

What We Is

Coats

The Whom Shrink

Lorry

Taking A Leak

Scooter Up!

Doctors Whom

Whom Whom

Eighties Guys

Slump

Is it just me or did it get really *busy* under the bridge?

There's not even anywhere to LEAN.

Maybe the mod movement has outgrown the bridge!

I don't see the point of having an elite society of tastemakers...

...if ANYBODY can join it.

JACK! HEY, JACK!

DOOT

What are you doing here?

We wanted to see what was going on.

Claire got wind that something big is going down today.

So we made t-shirts to protest.

Z Z

SO MOD

NOSTALGIA IS A DRUG

It'th TRUE!

YOU'RE ALL TOO TALL

New king incoming along with NEW QUEEN!

Knowing Jack's luck, it'll be Lauren again.

Or Shauna.

Knowing my luck, it'll be my ruddy MUM.

Good repartee, Jack. Definite level up.

WINK

+1 YEAH?

Oh my GAW it's CAMILLE.

So FRONCH. So STYLISH.

So EVIL!

Jack, you can look, it'th not your mum.

Praise be.

I bet Camille NEVER farts

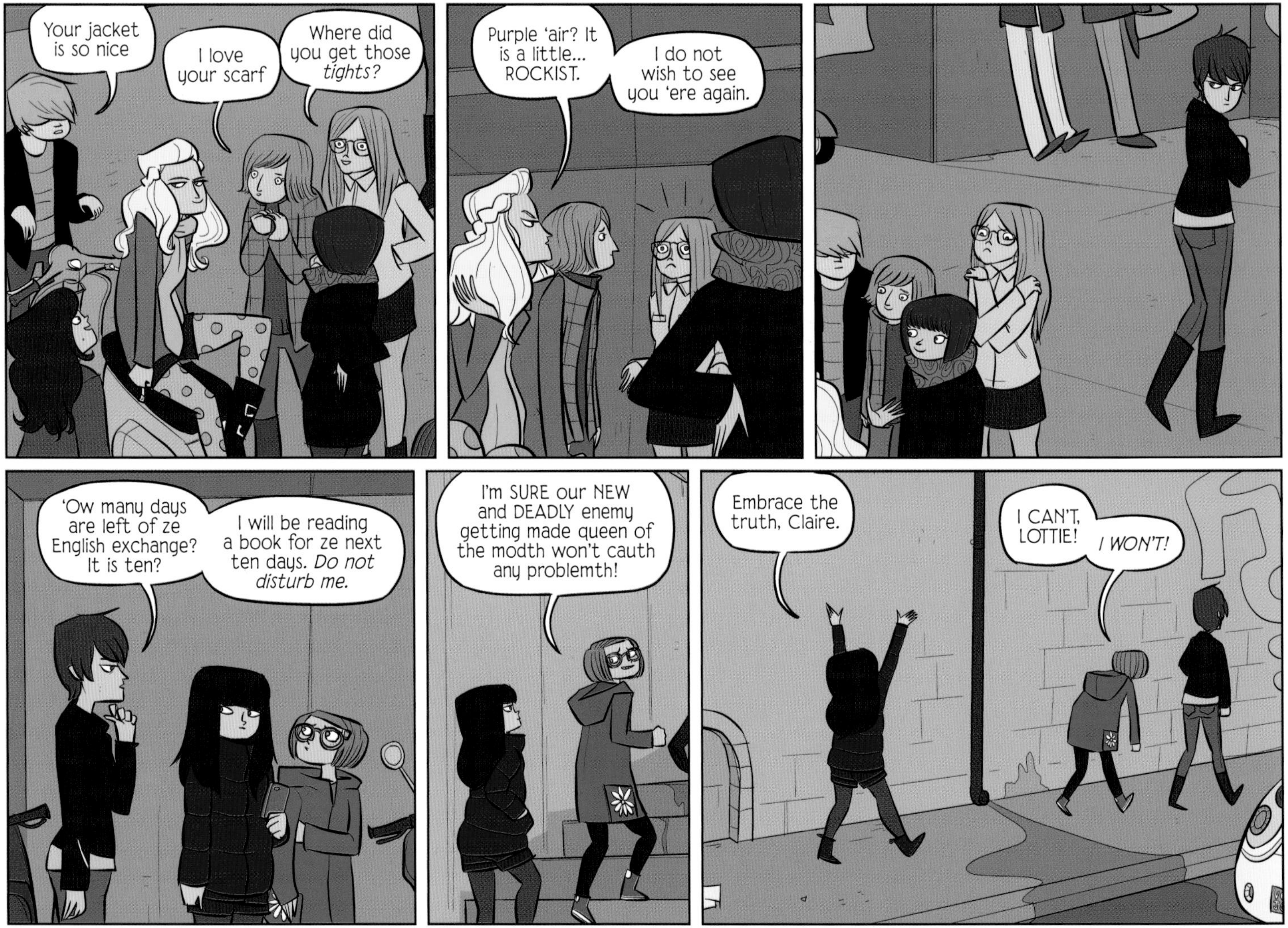
Your jacket is so nice
I love your scarf
Where did you get those *tights?*
Purple 'air? It is a little... ROCKIST.
I do not wish to see you 'ere again.
'Ow many days are left of ze English exchange? It is ten?
I will be reading a book for ze next ten days. *Do not disturb me.*
I'm SURE our NEW and DEADLY enemy getting made queen of the modth won't cauth any problemth!
Embrace the truth, Claire.
I CAN'T, LOTTIE!
I WON'T!

All zese DISQUES!

LA OH PO-KIPSY

Why is it that your friend Shauna is in a metal band and you are not?

Shauna likes to make fun of the black metal voice.

She's quite husky, she's too good at it.

UGG URG FURG WURG

WURG UG FUR HERRG

FINE-TIME FONTAINE IN LOVE

We should make a band. Wiz Claire.

FINE-TIME FONTAINE

No. No way. They'll want to put Claire on magazine covers on her own.

Too CUTE.

SMASH HITS
THE PANTONES
HISS
CLAIRE OF EGG BAND
+ MIMI + LOTTIE
SO CUTE

I AM NOT CUTE!

CRANG

First off you and me are only in the videos for five seconds, looking sideways...

Then she goes solo.

SOLO MOD

YOU DO LONG DIVISION ON MY HEAAAART

Claire Little, you stop having a music career right now!

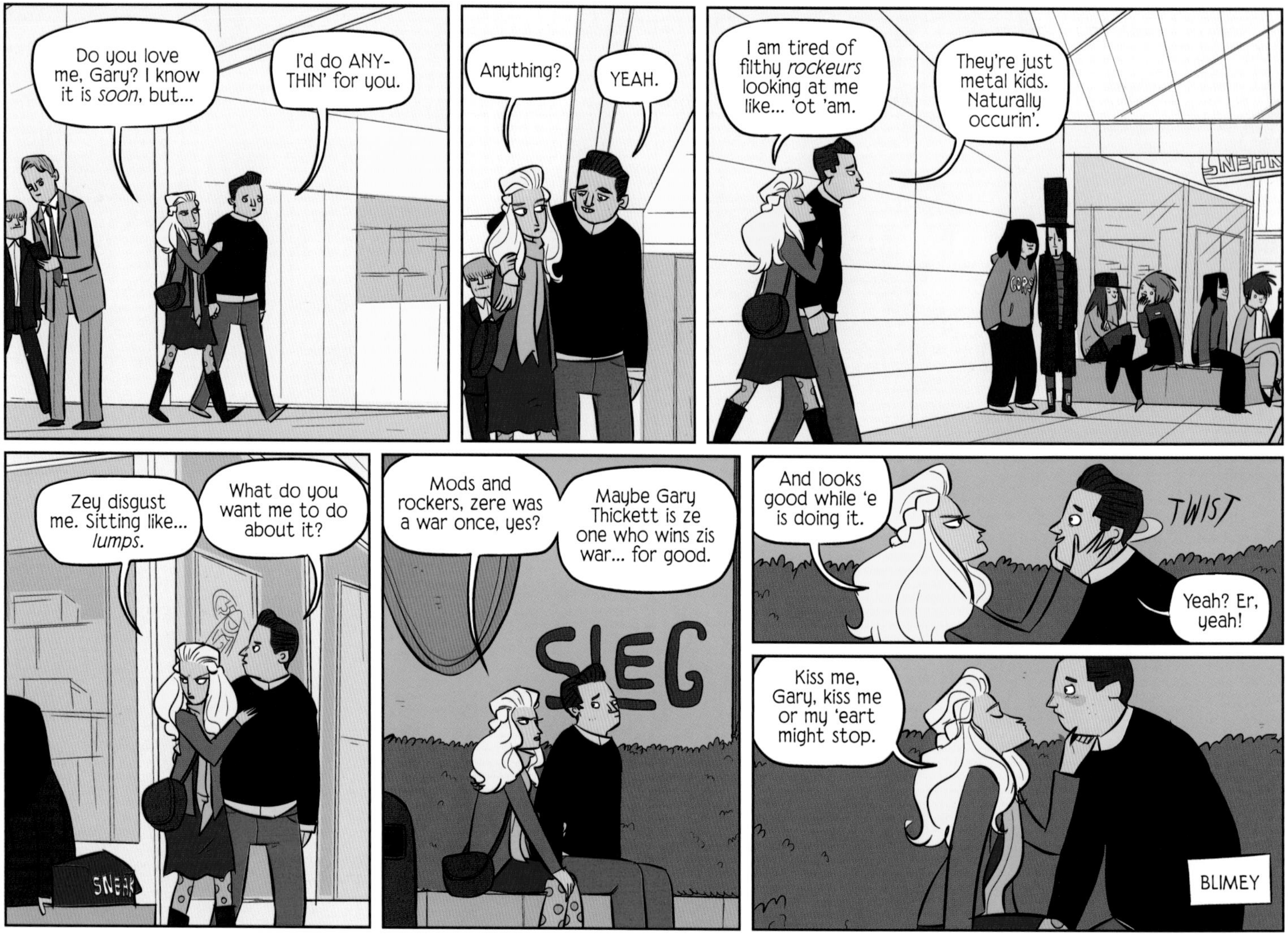
Do you love me, Gary? I know it is *soon*, but...
I'd do ANY-THIN' for you.
Anything?
YEAH.
I am tired of filthy *rockeurs* looking at me like... 'ot 'am.
They're just metal kids. Naturally occurin'.
Zey disgust me. Sitting like... *lumps*.
What do you want me to do about it?
Mods and rockers, zere was a war once, yes?
Maybe Gary Thickett is ze one who wins zis war... for good.
SIEG
And looks good while 'e is doing it.
TWIST
Yeah? Er, yeah!
Kiss me, Gary, kiss me or my 'eart might stop.
BLIMEY

What do you want me to do with these candlesticks, Amy?

Put them all out in the window. There's always money in candles.

Let's hope they never invent a more efficient way of lighting our homes.

Something weird's going on outside.

Hey! What do you think you're doing?

BANG BANG BANG

Clear the EFF OFF!

We're shutting early, Shauna.

Obviously not because we're scared in any way.

OPEN

Has this security shutter ever worked for you?

No. So PULL HARD!

And, um, try not to catch *tetanus*.

PANG PANG

Done! This old gal is tough!

Saw off the *Cabbage Patch Kid* riots of '83 without a scratch.

I'll give you a lift home, Shauna.

Come on Amy, there's menace in the air but we are TOUGH!

Sorry, I'm just worried about tonight. "Mr Beckwith" and I are having "company" over.

Worried why?

Apparently I need to "make friends".

Amy, you're COOL! You must have lots of friends!

I've got... friends.

But not the sort of friends who'd help you hide *crime evidence*.

MONGR3L
KNIFELAD
EPISIOTOMUS

Bell-Up
PHONE

Iggy mate I can't believe you got booted off stage by Tommy Fish.

LEGENDARY.

T-SHIRTS! HOODIES!

It's FREEZING. You wanna get some chips?

Nah, I'm skint.

What's the hold up?

I really want some chips.

Arrg, come on, we just wanna get past.

HOUSES BOUGHT QUICK CASH SALE CALL CHAZ 07141231

Are we trapped in a queue... to get beaten up?

There must be something we've learned playing video games that can get us out of this.

This gathering of Amalgamated Tackleford Mystery Solvers is called to order.

Apologia received in advance from Miss Mildred Haversham...

...who is currently undertaking Lord Bath's Excellence Awards.

Minutes today will be taken by Miss Shauna Wickle.

I've got a new pen!

Oh, that's nice.

Yeah, it's a gel pen, right?

But you can ERASE it.

Whoa.

I like that.

EXCUSE ME

DIG

ACCOUNTS CASES

SUPLISE

erase

We are here to investigate the rise of MOD and MOD-ON-ROCKER fights!

Not developments in stationery technology.

I'll look after THIS.

PLUCK

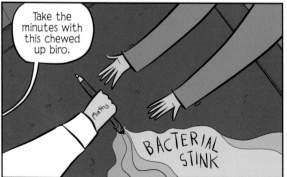

Take the minutes with this chewed up biro.

Maths

BACTERIAL STINK

You're safe with me.

Mods versus rockers is weird. It doesn't FIGURE.

In the sixties, rockers were violent toughs on a motorcycle.

Today they're just kids who like hairy music.

They're a peace-loving race.

I think they're quite... "sexist".

They're getting better!

"In the 1980s, bands like Iron Sod and Lünk were considered dangerous to women's delicate brain tissues".

"Today, scientists are not so sure".

IRON SOD

HMS BRASSIERE

LÜNK

TOUCH THE STEAK

Yeah! Girls have had to fight for the right to ROCK.

What website are you reading that on? "Barrypedia"?

It's *betterer*. More *authorititive*!

Is zis... 'ow you solved all ze mysteries in zese files?

It was EASIER when people didn't have so many OPINIONS.

CASE OF THE CRYSTAL CHILD

CASE OF THE BOXING DAY DANGER

Come on, Lottie, I think the boys have got the message.

Don't give yourself a migraine.

NGH!

BONK

I'm just well proud of our mystery-solving achievements.

Me too!

That shed stands for something.

Pubic boy minds can't change that.

Why do you 'old meetings in ze... shed?

It was my Grandpa's allotment, but he had a stroke and couldn't dig.

Lottie and me took it over.

Yes... I can tell zis.

It... it is a jungle?

Surely ze people of the ze "allotment" kick you off?

Such WEEDS.

PRIZE WINNING WEEDS.

Mimi, not wantin' to sound smug...

But we have so much DIRT on the allotment association.

This one? This is it?

They all look the same.

This is the one.

So, this place has to "cease to exist".

Flip. Okay.

PWEE

WAB

WAB

Fire engines! Maybe the mods are riotin'!

Zat would be on ze news. It is not on ze news.

POIROT

To Charlotte DENNIS FRANZ

I'm scared of riots.

Rioting is a great French tradition, Charlotte, like pastry. And affairs.

Une baguette, it is 'ard so we can throw it through a shop window.

Lottie. *Lottie.* LOTTIE.

Who... who could have done this?

All our CASE NOTES... all our RECORDS... everything!

Gone!

Could it have been... the allotment association?

They wouldn't DARE.

Zis was Camille. I know it.

We'll get her, Lottie.

No we won't. This is a sign. An OMEN.

No more cases. I'm out. I'm gonna dress in black and embrace darkness.

Lottie!!

It's CHARLOTTE.

"Lottie" died with the mystery shed, Shauna.

If you want to talk to her, buy a *ouija board*.

Are you... the fire investigator?

What do you think happened? Arson?

Three bar electric fire. Probably left on overnight. WOOSH. Textbook.

But... we NEVER leave the fire on! We check!

All it would take is some very dry seeds to fall on to the bars...

Classic allotment blaze.

DON

Run along to school, girls.

Don't patronise me! I'm traumatised!

I smell petrol. Can you not?

Someone's probably growing *bio fuel*. It's very popular nowadays.

ZIS IS A PETROL CAN.

Well don't wave it around, everybody'll want one.

BWO EEE

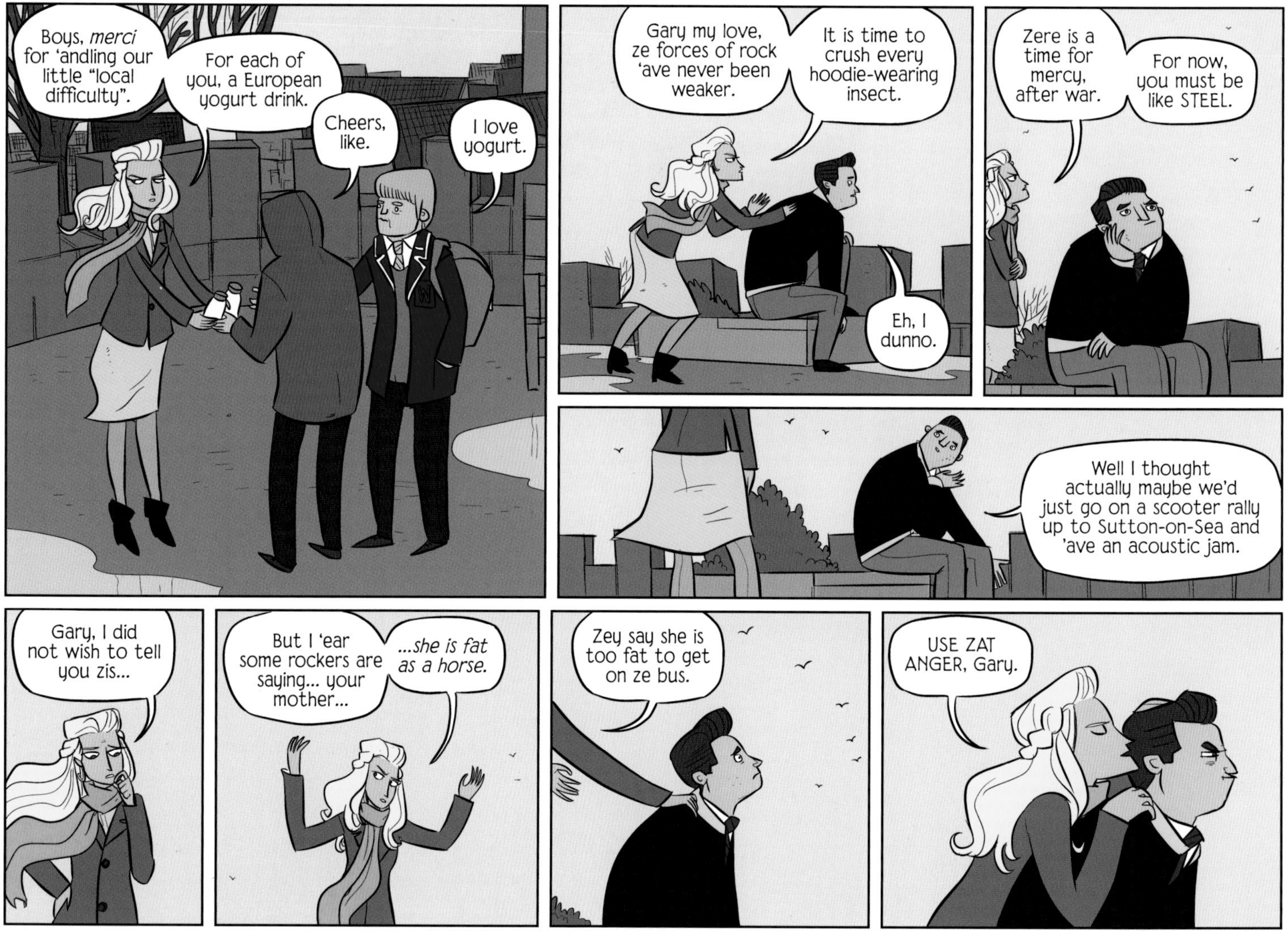
Boys, *merci* for 'andling our little "local difficulty".
For each of you, a European yogurt drink.
Cheers, like.
I love yogurt.
Gary my love, ze forces of rock 'ave never been weaker.
It is time to crush every hoodie-wearing insect.
Eh, I dunno.
Zere is a time for mercy, after war.
For now, you must be like STEEL.
Well I thought actually maybe we'd just go on a scooter rally up to Sutton-on-Sea and 'ave an acoustic jam.
Gary, I did not wish to tell you zis...
But I 'ear some rockers are saying... your mother...
...she is fat as a horse.
Zey say she is too fat to get on ze bus.
USE ZAT ANGER, Gary.

I came as quick as I could, Mimi!

Shauna! She is in the garden going CRAZY!

What are you doing?

Stay out of my way, Wickle.

CHUCK

Lottie, you can't burn all your puffer jackets!

THE PAST IS DUST.

Are you burning your mystery scrapbooks too?

Don't do that!

It doesn't matter any more.

You're my best friend in the world! I won't let you keep doing this!

Let go of me Shauna.

I have to put the grass back before mum gets home.

Charlotte?

Let us go out. Tonight is an exchange activity. *Cinema.* Culture.

I don't feel well.

I cannot believe zis beats you. It is PATHETIC.

You're pathetic, yeah? ZING.

SLAM

Hi Mimi. What are you doing?

Nothing.

Do you 'ave another cigarette?

No, sorry.

Zat is okay.

You still 'ave a shop of disques! So cool!

There aren't many little ones left. We're lucky here.

I like coming here, even though I can't afford to buy anything.

You can listen to it all for free on the computer, but it's not the same, Mimi.

Non non, when you buy it, you try 'ard to like it, yes?

I love ze SMELL!

So NASTY!

Would you like something in the cafe?

Ohh... I've not got any money on me.

I will buy you a *boisson*, poor English boy.

EVERYBODY IS LOOKING AT ME.

EVERY-BODY.

Jack, are you... afraid of 'ot choco-late?

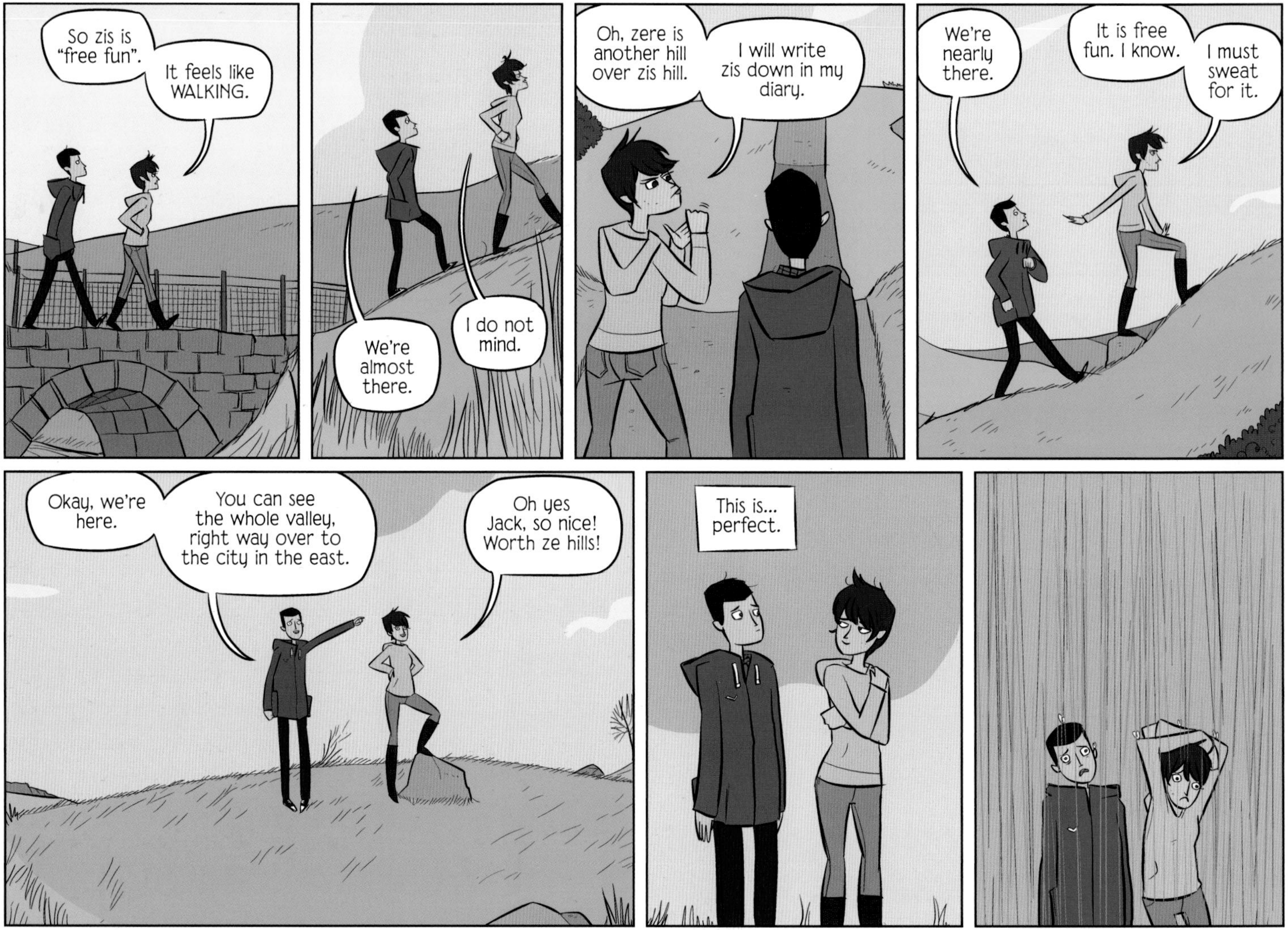
So zis is "free fun".
It feels like WALKING.
We're almost there.
I do not mind.
Oh, zere is another hill over zis hill.
I will write zis down in my diary.
We're nearly there.
It is free fun. I know.
I must sweat for it.
Okay, we're here.
You can see the whole valley, right way over to the city in the east.
Oh yes Jack, so nice! Worth ze hills!
This is... perfect.

Sorry about the rain. There'll be a bus soon. Soon-ish.

Yes, Yorkshire and its rain. Very rain. Most rain.

I reckon if Britain could export its rain to dryer countries...

...we'd all be rich.

Eh?

WHY DO I SAY *ANYTHING*?

Bus is here already!

Must've been the last one, running late.

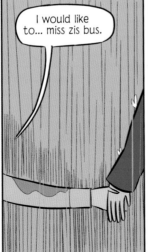

I would like to... miss zis bus.

What's going on? There are mods and rockers everywhere.

It feels like... there's going to be a fight.

Put your 'ood on, Jack. You are very mod with zat 'air.

My papa says, when you see people in long trousers running outdoors...

...it is time to be *indoors*.

We can get the X12 over there, it goes near Lottie's house and mine.

BWAP

CHILD PASS

Is zis... a common sight?

No... I'd say you only see someone using a flying V as a battle axe on special occasions.

Charlotte.

I 'ad an afternoon most incredible with Jack and saw ze town going CRAZY.

Lottie?

What are you listening to?

What is zis? Ze drone that goes beyond time and space?

One chord a minute. Music without JOY.

Oh Lottie it is ze most JOY day of all time.

I kissed Jack and...

You kissed Jack? How did it feel?

I felt like ELECTRICITY! Never more ALIVE!

It was ze first time.

I remember feeling alive.

SNAP

The Case of the Modern Men

Shop windows were smashed and several shops gutted by fire...

LANCE WILBERFORCE
Youth Fracas Correspondent
BBC NEWS 19·01

...as mod-rocker violence spread throughout Tackleford city centre.

Police were called-

19:02:30

Come on love, you shouldn't be watching this.

See if Lottie wants her tea.

Hey, BRIDE OF DEATH, your *diner* est PRET.

Not hungry. I am a wraith now.

My papa and sister both teach the English...

...but I do not know zis "wraith".

Basic ghost, yeah?

Ah yes. Ze ghost of a a girl who 'ad eight purple puffer jackets of different sizes...

...and did not care what anyody thought of 'er.

The memories are HAZY...

...but if it is sausages for tea...

...maybe I will draw strength from their PORKEN STEAM.

MARCH

Years of tradition, Lauren, all gone.

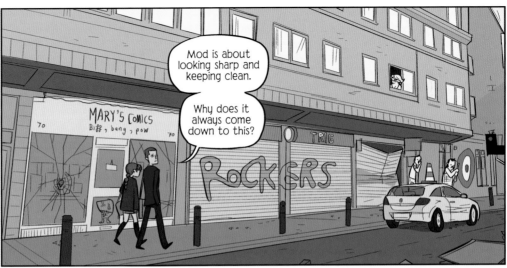

Mod is about looking sharp and keeping clean.

Why does it always come down to this?

Ace Face suits... destroyed.

Rod's Italian café - badly bashed in.

Club de Jazz... all sicked up on the steps.

In fairness, that might not have been done by rockers.

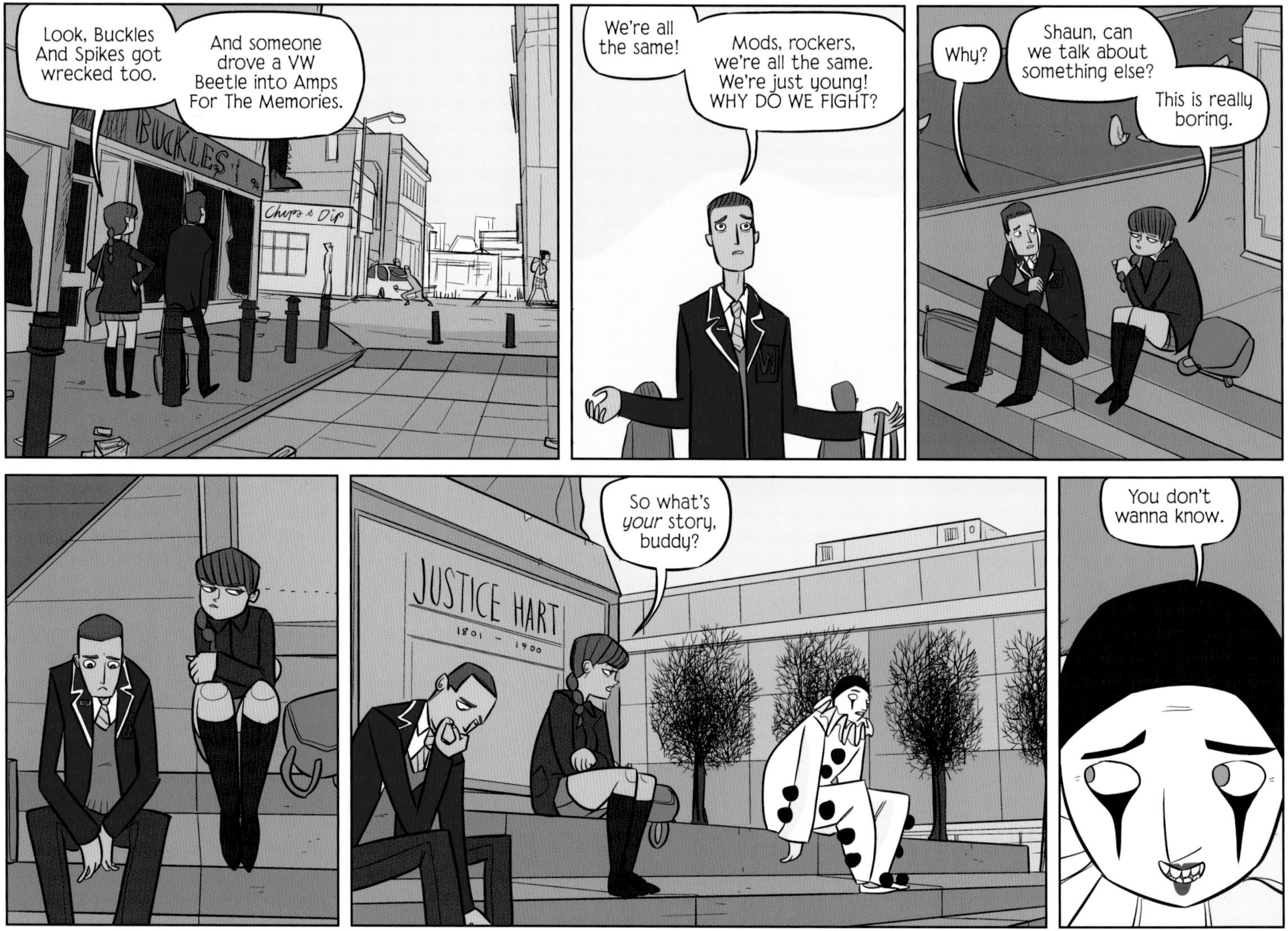
Look, Buckles And Spikes got wrecked too.
And someone drove a VW Beetle into Amps For The Memories.
BUCKLES
Chips & Dip
We're all the same!
Mods, rockers, we're all the same. We're just young! WHY DO WE FIGHT?
Why?
Shaun, can we talk about something else?
This is really boring.
JUSTICE HART
1801 – 1900
So what's *your* story, buddy?
You don't wanna know.

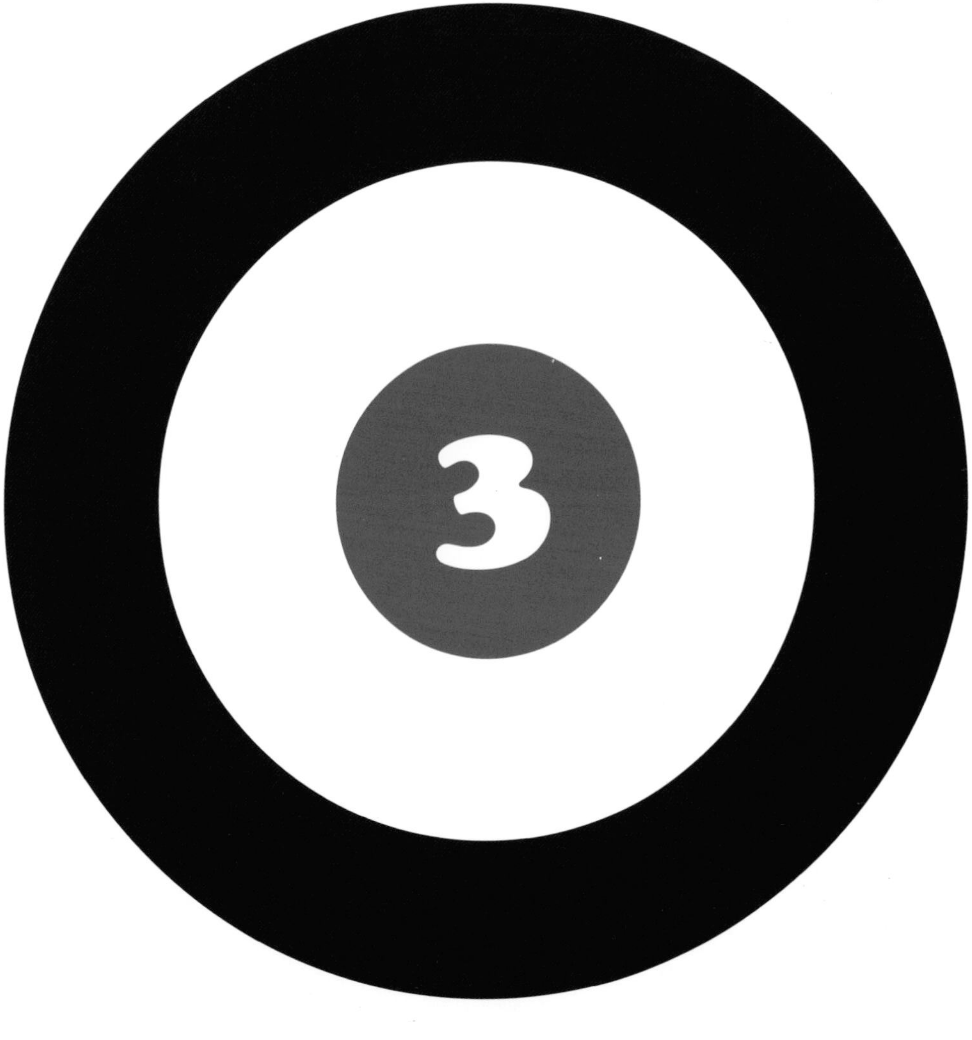
3

Hey, what's going on?

I'm here for band practice! I've got three new songs, well growly!

Practice is off, Shauna.

We're makin' his drums into a siege engine for fighting the mods.

Shut up Rod, we said we weren't gonna tell 'er.

You're fighting the mods? I wanna fight too! I'm TOUGH!

You'll get your face kicked in.

This is because I'm a GIRL!

J'ACCUSE

I am ROCK! I will FIGHT!

Two votes to one, you're out of Brutalism UK. You're not rock any more.

Go home.

WHAT?

We could have been so big, Rod.

JOAN OF ARC WAS A GIRL!

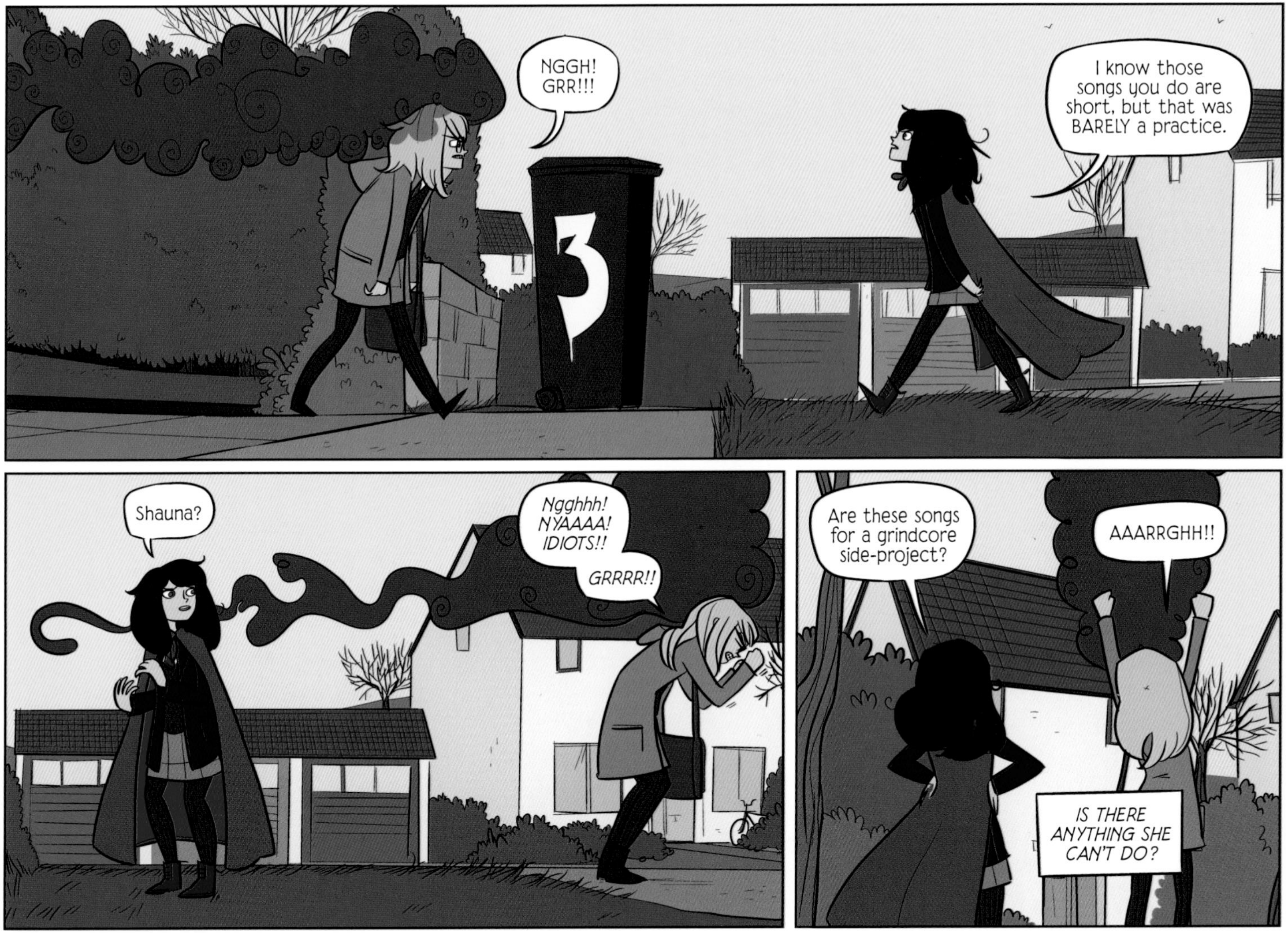
NGGH! GRR!!!
I know those songs you do are short, but that was BARELY a practice.
Shauna?
Ngghhh! NYAAAA! IDIOTS!!
GRRRR!!
Are these songs for a grindcore side-project?
AAARRGHH!!
IS THERE ANYTHING SHE CAN'T DO?

Ladies and "gentlemen", we are going to solve this last case.

What... what happened to Lottie?

She swore off her GHDs.

She'll regret it when a family of mice start living in there.

Shauna and Linton, go and map out mod and rocker territory.

Oh WHAT, that's like *homework*.

Bring back Mildred, she had a nerd's love of maps. *So unfair.*

Jack, you well love the old mod king, go and ask him to do something useful.

I DO NOT LOVE HIM.

Sonny, you and I will find out how a dim bulb called Gary can send a town mad.

We will AVENGE the mystery shed.

Don't they say, if you go looking for vengeance, dig two graves?

Then hire a field and a JCB, Sonny.

I predict HEAVY VENGE.

Where's Mimi?

She's being "made to see a castle".

You're not in love with her too, are you?

Only a bit. I mean er, NO.

Well, you're too late. Your mate Jack done did kisses with her.

Ohhh.

Now, as we suspected, Gary Thickett is having a flamenco guitar lesson.

He almost looks... peaceful.

Gary's just a blunt knife with a moped.

Queen Mod Camille's behind all the mayhem.

Do you think... you provoked her... a bit?

Maybe, but I think people at school would have been queuing up to hand that cowbag a fart sandwich.

I can't believe he got that lovely scooter ahead of me. So nice. So... nice.

Go on, sit on it. He'll never know.

Imagine the tingle.

Um, excuse me?

How can I help?

I was just wondering which budgie seed is best? *Trill* or *Cheep*?

They're exactly the same.

It's... heh... ironic isn't it? "Cheep" is slightly more expensive.

Are you wasting my time for a bet?

No, er, Sean, I was wondering if you'd help end the mod-rocker war.

The old king, back in the saddle.

I don't do that stuff any more.

Oh.

I'm... a friend of Lauren's?

Mate, I really need to stack this pile of stuff for vermin to defecate onto.

The Case of the Modern Men

I'm not sitting on it. It wouldn't be right.

Sonny, you are so good. Too good.

SWOOP

It gives off a soft sort of glow.

Uh, I don't think... wait yeah it does kind of!

Do you think maybe the BIKE is causing the mod-rocker war?

Well, it's far fetched.

But no more far fetched than Gary Thickett leading a ruddy youth army.

It's a really old bike.

Maybe it's cursed. Or "en-chanted". Or Satan rode it once...

...in the nude.

The log book for the bike will say who owned it last.

How the flipping flip do we get hold of that?

I have an idea.

If the idea involves a virtual reality helmet, I will endorse it sight unseen.

He's finishing his guitar lesson!

Okay Lottie, my plan to get the log book off Gary involves you standing... over there.

Over here?

Yes.

Oh lore what is he saying to him? That boy and his "exchanges"!!

STLE

Grr! Turn *around!*

AND?

The previous owner of the bike was Lee Lorson of 71, North Parade.

POP
POP
POP

Maybe we can ask him who he bought it from.

How U do dat, Sonny?

He told me! He's just a lad who likes scooters!

I KNEW IT. Camille *is* the power behind the throne.

She bewitched that sap.

Well, she is heavily perfumed.

It's quite a musk.

SCRAP
BOUGHT
+
SOLD
€A$H

Grandpa Joe's on the phone to the DVLA!

Tommy Swale... Donald Braddock... Wesley Piper, Lee Lorson.

Right, thanks very much.

Well Sonny, that scooter you liked...

...was owned by the four most legendary ace faces Tackleford has ever seen.

CLING!

I knew it! I knew it! That bike is special!

Special? Cursed more like.

Tommy Swale was king of the mods in 1963.

He was so good looking, he modelled for Italian Vogue.

He was hit by a freak wave on Brighton Pier.

All they found was his skull.

Those... cheekbones.

Donald Braddock was king in '67. Big on silk scarves and paisley.

Now, I wouldn't like to say he was "decapitated"...

...but he did end up... sort of stopping at the shoulders.

OPEN

Wesley Piper, "the hairy mod", rose up the ranks quick. He was king by '76.

While medicine had made great leaps, it proved ill-matched to the challenge...

... of reat-taching Piper's head to his spine.

WHAT

H-h-h-how?

Wes was well into CB radio.

He invented a special CB helmet, which sadly exploded on the A59 to Ingleton.

And Lee Lorson?

Mid nineties mod king. Check shirt, wet look gel.

Please tell me he wasn't beheaded in a freak accident.

All right, I won't.

But for the sake of completeness...

...we should be open to the idea?

It just fell off.

No explanation.

Sonny, I am well scared, there are mods everywhere.

It's gonna be another bad night.

My dad says, when you're worried, walk confidently.

And that's probably easier for you than me, you came to school in a cape today.

Do you think King Gary's scooter is actually cursed?

Er, yeah! The most cursed!

First it makes you a powerful king.

Then...

OFF WITH YOUR HEAD!

And do you think we can stop Gary... going "topless"?

It's 50/50 I reckon. I can't be sure he'll come out of this with... *all his ears.*

What happened in Tackleford on Thursday night was ROCK'S DARKEST HOUR.

Metalheads, moshers, heshers, punks and head-bangers made MINCEMEAT BY MODS.

Who are you?

I am LEILA TAYLOR! I am here from BIRMINGHAM

...to save you.

Whoa what, the national city of ROCK.

They've got scooters, they can move faster than us, love.

I AM NOT YOUR "LOVE".

You will sell your guitars and buy MOTORBIKES.

We 'aven't got us compulsory basic training.

YOU WILL GET IT!

There's a waiting list!

TOSS

I HAVE BLOCK-BOOKED THE BIKE SCHOOL TOMORROW!

BRING A PACKED LUNCH!

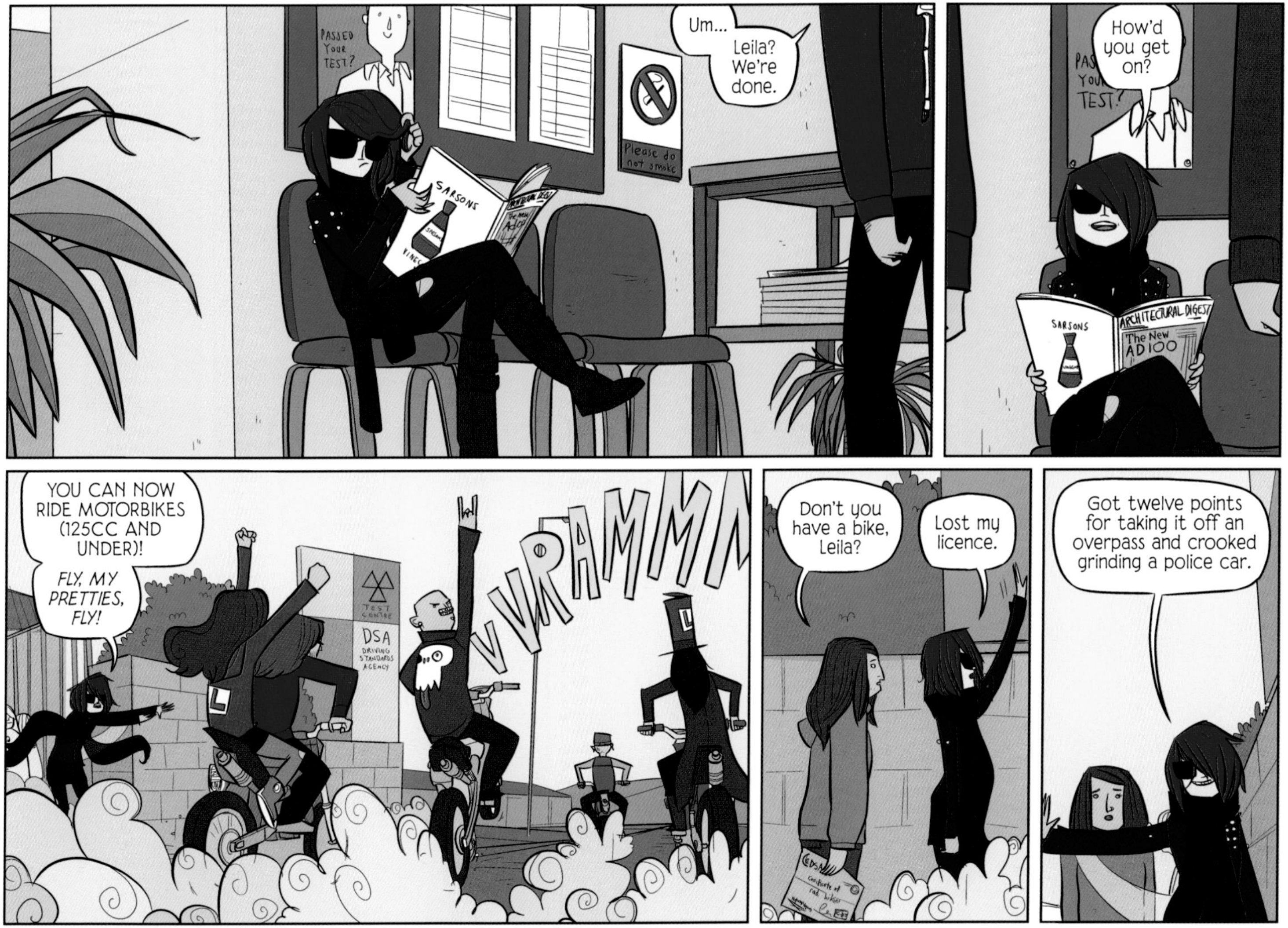
PASSED YOUR TEST?
Please do not smoke
Um...
Leila? We're done.
SARSONS
ARCHITECTURAL DIGEST
The New AD100
How'd you get on?
YOU CAN NOW RIDE MOTORBIKES (125CC AND UNDER)!
FLY, MY PRETTIES, FLY!
TEST CENTRE
DSA DRIVING STANDARDS AGENCY
VVRAMMM
Don't you have a bike, Leila?
Lost my licence.
Got twelve points for taking it off an overpass and crooked grinding a police car.

A second night of violence saw "rockers", now on motorbikes, attack several mod targets...

...including an upscale cobblers and the Bevis comb factory.

Skirmishes took place until the early hours, with several black eyes reported.

Enough, Lauren.

A mate of yours came to me, skinny lad.

Jack. Said he had a plan.

What plan could Jack have? End the war with cute trembling?

Hey, *Finch.*

GULP

Sean says, whatever you need him to do, he'll do it.

Oh! Okay!

So, did you kiss that French girl yet?

Um... um...

OH MY GOD.

YOU *RASCAL.*

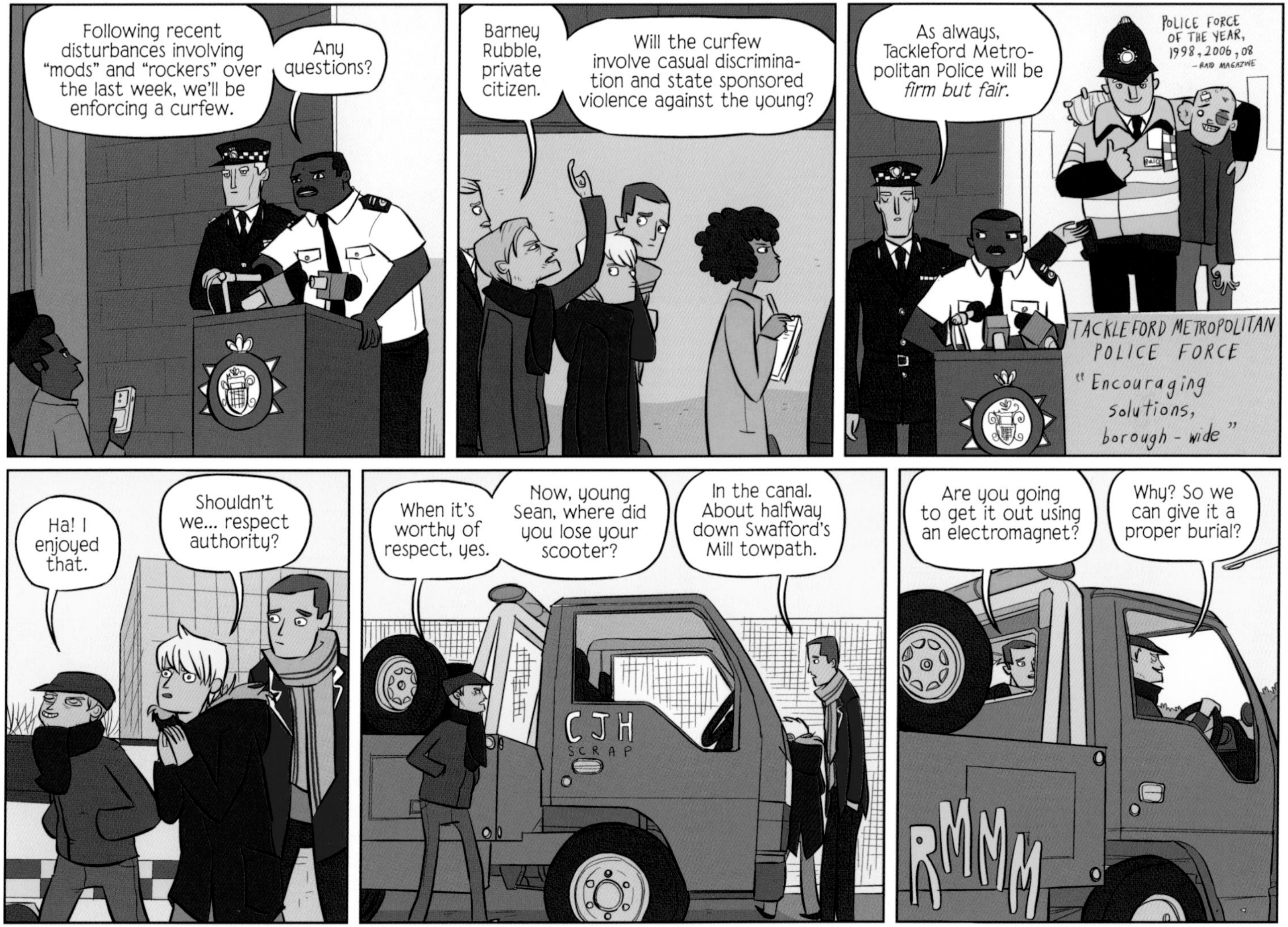
Following recent disturbances involving "mods" and "rockers" over the last week, we'll be enforcing a curfew.
Any questions?
Barney Rubble, private citizen.
Will the curfew involve casual discrimination and state sponsored violence against the young?
As always, Tackleford Metropolitan Police will be *firm but fair.*
POLICE FORCE OF THE YEAR, 1998, 2006, 08 - RAD MAGAZINE
TACKLEFORD METROPOLITAN POLICE FORCE
"Encouraging solutions, borough-wide"
Ha! I enjoyed that.
Shouldn't we... respect authority?
When it's worthy of respect, yes.
Now, young Sean, where did you lose your scooter?
In the canal. About halfway down Swafford's Mill towpath.
CJH SCRAP
Are you going to get it out using an electromagnet?
Why? So we can give it a proper burial?
RMMM

The Case of the Modern Men

All right lad, here you go. I was fixing this up for Sonny, but...

You were fixing it up for me?

Oh Sonny, mate, I can't take your bike.

No no. It's important. You're the only one who can stop this war.

You're sure?

Yes.

That's...

VREEE

...the taste I remember.

HITCH

Sonny, I'm proud of you.

But a word to the wise...

If this situation arises with a girl instead of a bike...

...knock the other feller out.

An old-fashioned challenge for king of the mods.

Blood in the air, rubber on the road.

Reminds me of when men were men and tattoos were *exclusively nautical.*

What challenge are you going to go for, Sean?

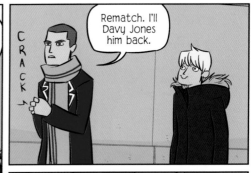

Rematch. I'll Davy Jones him back.

You're a fool.

You'll be right back in the drink.

You need to wipe this punk out. He can never be king again.

That means... THE JIMMY CLITHEROE.

The "Jimmy Clitheroe"?

A three-part ace face-off to test the mettle of even the sharpest mod.

Wait here!

This is very exciting, Grandpa!

Quick Sonny, help me make up what the Jimmy Clitheroe is.

Your Grandpa Joe got a bit over-excited in the heat of the moment.

The Case of the Modern Men

LITTLE RESIDENCE

The world ith *thad* and I feel bad...

Punch me out like a hanging *chad*

I ought to write that down.

Quite PUNK.

HISS
SUPREMACY TOUR

Maybe you two can cheer her up.

She's been spending a lot of time aggressively strummng up there.

Claire, your friends are here.

Are you doing all right living with the mod queen?

Yeth... we came to an underthtanding.

I underthtand that I should stay in my room and be VERY QUIET.

She underthandth that she can use all my shampoo and take my memory foam pillow.

Memorieth of it... *are all I have left.*

GARY THICKETT! I CHALLENGE YOU!

Come on mate, don't be daft. You've lost one bike already.

Actually, Gary, you can't refuse a challenge. It's the rules.

Who's your second?

I forgot that I needed a second.

Flip. *Flip.*

No second and your challenge is void, Sean.

Rules.

I'll do it.

Jack, have you lost your marbles?

You've never even ridden a scooter.

Jack, zis is... *crazy!* Tell them you did not mean it!

He probably won't have to do anything, Mimi.

And if he does, he'll probably die in the process, so it won't bother him *long-term.*

PAT PAT

CHALLENGE ACCEPTED!

It's the police! It's curfew time!

I'd fight them but I've got to revise this evening.

I promised my gran I'd wash her net curtains for her...

...otherwise I'd *well* be fighting the police.

OOF!

SCREECH

POLICE

That's dad's new non-lethal weapons unit.

He's tried a few of them on me and my brothers.

I love your dad, Linton.

Posterior Active Denial System (PADS) - makes you feel like your bum's on fire.

Concentrated Instagram filter... pacifies crowds with a sense of nostalgic peace.

Immobilising foam - dry cleaning NIGHTMARE

And that's just a spork.

But in the right hands... *non-lethal.*

What in God's name are they all up to up there?

I don't know, but that awful Grote girl is wearing a cape now.

Watch out for that diabolical creature, Tom.

I forsee her ruining our Christmas dinners for decades to come.

Nope. Nothing yet.

Refresh, Jack, refresh.

I just refreshed.

F5

Maybe it's cached.

Maybe YOU'RE cached, Linton.

I've been invited to a new Facebook event.

"MOD KING CHALLENGE".

PWIP

Reply "maybe".

Don't look too keen.

Where's Shauna?

The former king of the mods is here!

TS-E-AN!

RA RA RA!

MOD KING LA!

Well, you let this one get quite out of hand, didn't you, Sonny?

AND I LOVE IT.

SQUEAK SQUEAK

SQUEAK

That's Sean's second? Jack Finch?

SQUEAK

They say he's got an amazing amount of guts.

Occupying the space where a brain would usually be.

GARY'S THE ONE

SQUEAK SQUEAK

UP YR GAZ

Are you ready, Sean?

Sort of. Just give me a minute.

He's either got very efficient kidneys, or the bladder of a sparrow.

I hope I'm not ruining the MOD MYSTIQUE.

PHEW.

TINKLE TINKLE ZIP

Right. TIME TO WIN.

Surely the once and future King of the Mods would wash his hands, Sean.

You're right, Padre. Very poor form.

SKWWK

CLOG

Padre, as a man of God, you surprise me.

Never took a vow, Camille.

I just like the threads.

Where's Sean? He's been ten minutes.

I don't know. He's not answering his phone.

Sean Finnigan is a no-show.

His second must take the challenge.

Seriously, Finch, there's no shame in ducking out.

CHALLENGE ACCEPTED.

GARY GARY GARY GAR

GARY'S SO GAGEAR

JOHN 3:16

THICKETT CAN NICK IT

LOVE U GAZ

JACK JAC JACK JACK JA

And the challenge is... *the Jimmy Clitheroe?*

What's that?

It's a three-part challenge comprising a theory portion, a style-off, and a race-off.

It's legendary. I can't imagine you'd not have heard of it.

Of course I have!

He bought it!

And you gave Jack all the answers to the theory questions, yeah?

Well that wouldn't have been fair.

The Case of the Modern Men

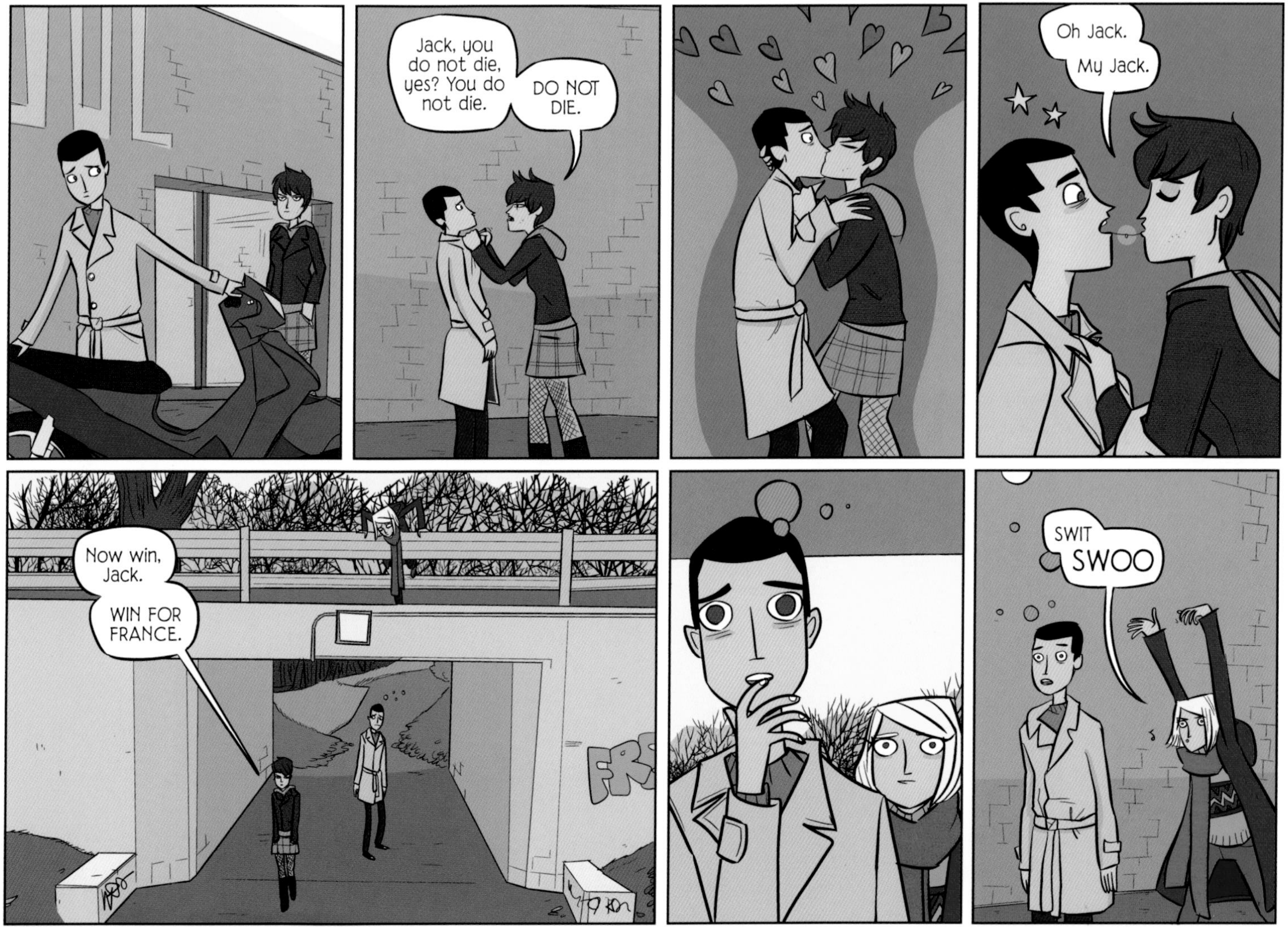
Jack, you do not die, yes? You do not die.
DO NOT DIE.
Oh Jack.
My Jack.
Now win, Jack.
WIN FOR FRANCE.
SWIT
SWOO

1. When folding a pocket square, how many points should be visible between Whitsun and Advent?

Trick question – you don't wear a pocket square after Whitsun

4. When courting a girl, how should one show one's first romantic intentions?

Offer to lend her a trad jazz "78" record

11. The traditional mod stance is feet 8 inches apart, one hand in pocket – excepting which circumstances?

When standing on a gradient of greater than 3 in 1

21. Who is considered the first, or "alpha" mod?

SNAP

The 13th Lord Sunderland

This is so easy!

TURN

WHAT?

How do I answer this?

SCRIBBLE
SCRIBBLE
SCRIBBLE
SCRIBBLE
SCRIBBLE
SCRIBBLE

Jack, the answer to "which Whom album is best?" is "Taking A Leak".

Not "The Whom are garbage music".

Gary Thickett 1
Jack Finch 0

To be a true aesthetic modernist, a FACE, style must be INTRINSIC.

Fashion can be faked, but true style cannot be denied.

Two-time Miss Yorkshire Betty Rubble is sitting at that window.

How you walk past her limpid gaze will test every drop of style in you.

Watch and learn.

FL

IP

BOW

Gary Thickett 1
Jack Finch 1

Finch, it's pretty obvious that even when you lose, you've got more class than me.

Thanks, Gary!

Can I ask... you seem reasonable...

...why don't you just stop the mod-rocker war?

It's Camille... it's out of my hands.

DRUM DRUM

If I did, she'd just... she'd replace me.

Gary, people are waiting for you to CRUSH zis worm.

If he's a worm... I'm a slightly shorter worm.

CLAP

Take me to the next place, Gary, take me there fast.

I shouldn't really razz it up, Cammy, the engine's not made to-

Take me there so fast.

Razzzzzzzz

The final challenge is a 3-lap race of the old Horslips warehouse site.

CLANK

Isn't the chequered flag how you end a race, not start it?

It's my mums old tablecloth. Why are you wearing a cape?

GAR GAR
JACK JACK JACK JACK

3-2-1

START

Go!

It won't go!

BLONK

Oh nuts.

Too much razzing it up.

Easy, Jack, easy.

BOOT

START

Just get round this first bend, then we'll try double figures.

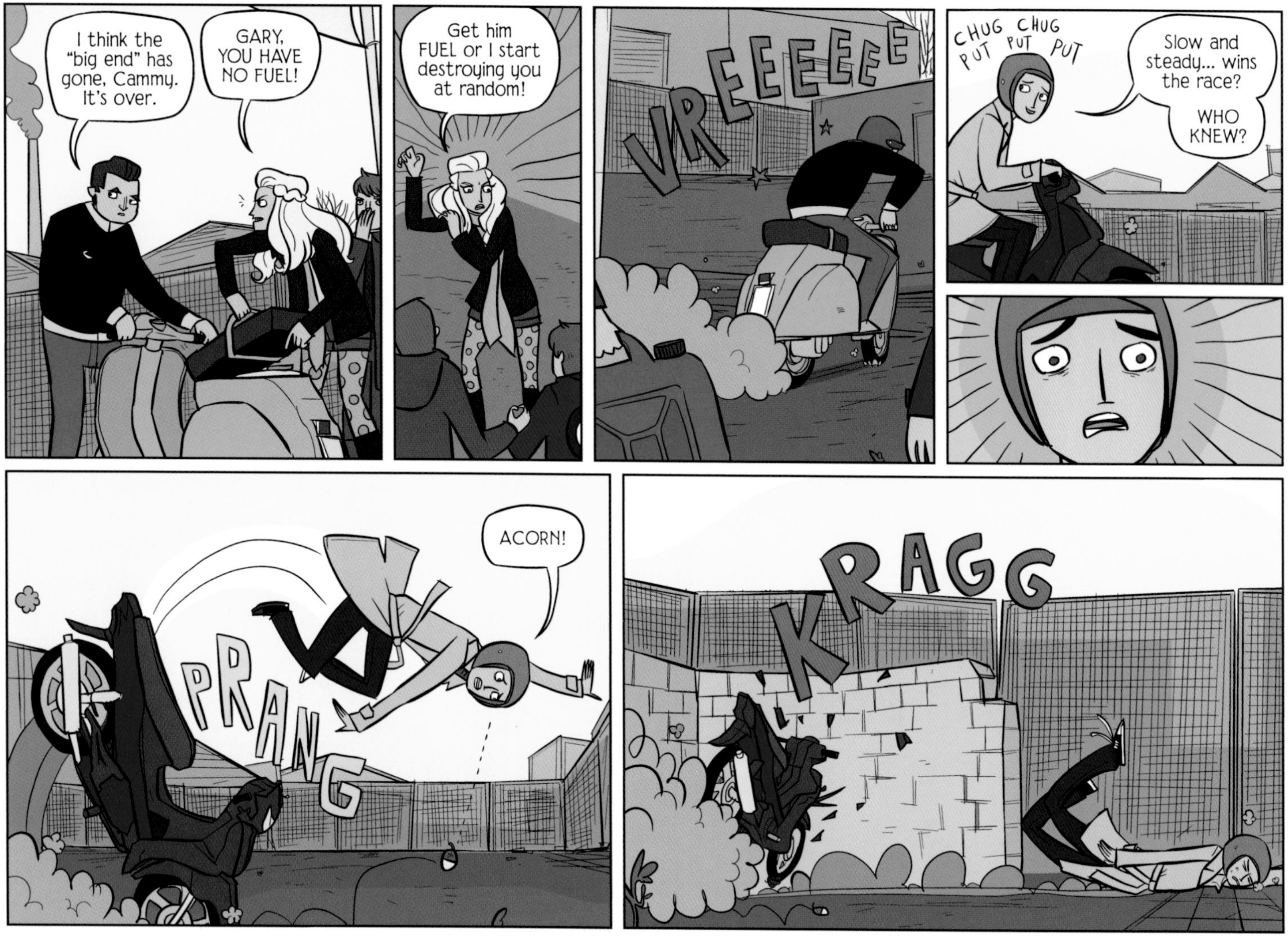
I think the "big end" has gone, Cammy. It's over.
GARY, YOU HAVE NO FUEL!
Get him FUEL or I start destroying you at random!
VREEEEEE
CHUG CHUG PUT PUT PUT
Slow and steady... wins the race?
WHO KNEW?
ACORN!
PRANG
KRAGG

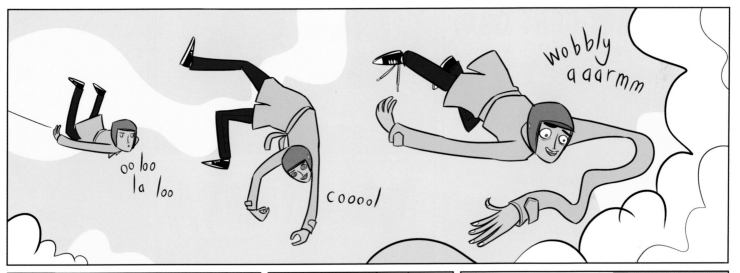

oo loo la loo

cooool

wobbly aaarmm

Jack, are you okay?

I'm in heaven, and you're all here!

Just like... in the movies?

No Jack, you fell off the scooter.

CLAW

Got to win!

I'm sorry to report that the component parts of your scooter...

...are now thrivin' independently of each other.

The Case of the Modern Men

Beautiful, ain't it?

Yeah. A classic.

Magic condition too.

They don't make 'em like this any more.

Sigh.

WHACK

BOOT

WHACK

BOOT

GLOOK GLOOK

It seems such an awful waste. *Such a lovely bike.*

The last fashionable idiot has lost his head on that demon cycle.

Bury the bits so no one can make an *amulet!*

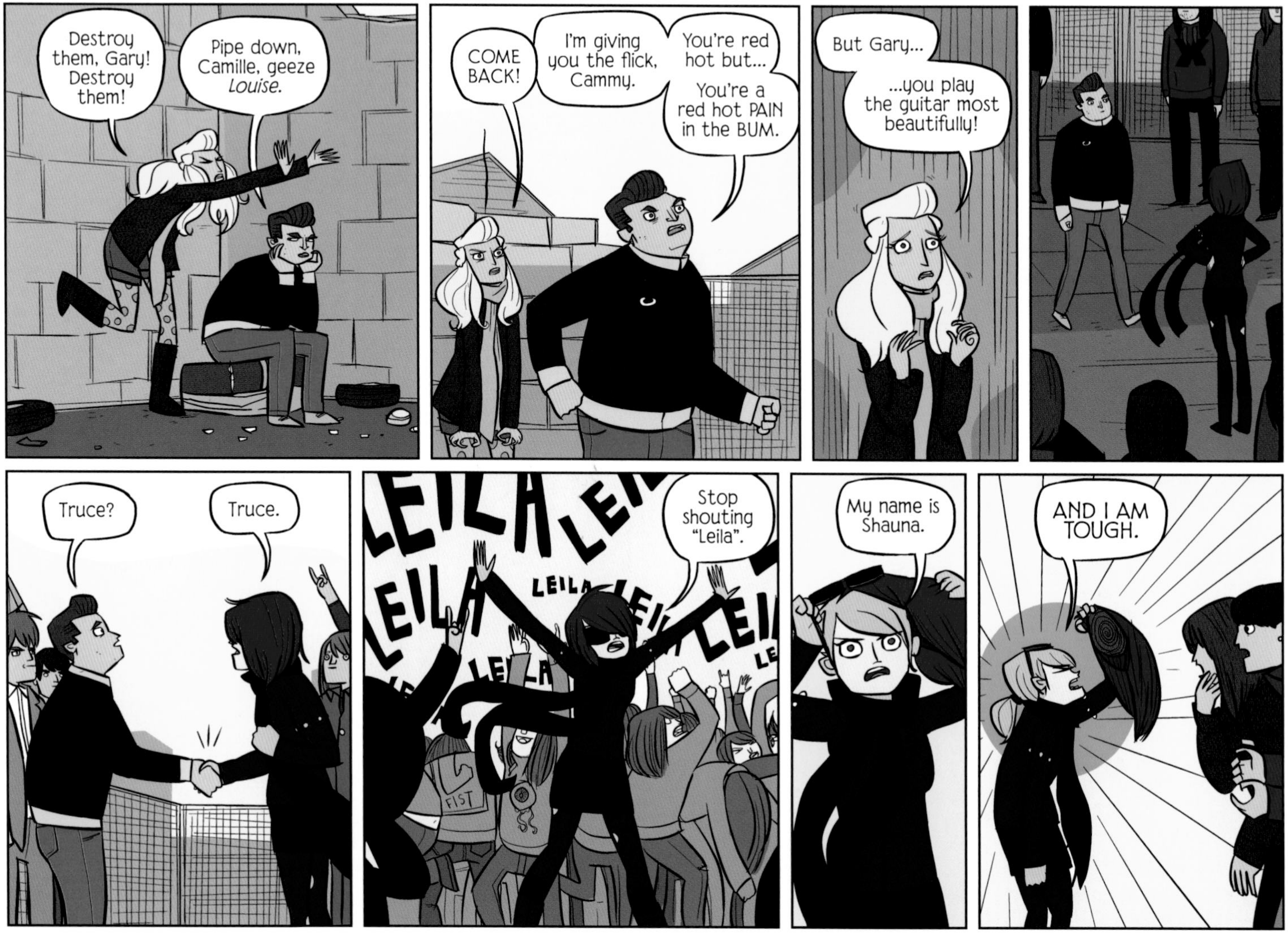
Destroy them, Gary! Destroy them!
Pipe down, Camille, geeze *Louise.*
COME BACK!
I'm giving you the flick, Cammy.
You're red hot but...
You're a red hot PAIN in the BUM.
But Gary...
...you play the guitar most beautifully!
Truce?
Truce.
LEILA
LEILA
LEILA
FIST
Stop shouting "Leila".
My name is Shauna.
AND I AM TOUGH.

Shauna, that was so BADASS, omigod.

This was going to be my on-stage costume.

At least I got to use it for something.

You're quitting powerviolence? Maybe going crustcore?

Nah, it all gives me a sore throat. No more music.

Where are Jack and Mimi going?

She's leaving tomorrow. It's very sad.

Tragic Fronch-style romance.

Mimi...

Jack, we cannot say what will be.

So we will say nothing.

It's been nice.

Yes. Very nice.

I thought you were meant to be *tough*, Shauna.

Shut up, Lottie.

CLICK

Camille, I think that while you have been here...

...I have been A VERY GOOD HOTHT.

And you have not been very PLEATHANT to me.

But if you have not learned how to be PLEATHANT by the time I come to VITHIT...

...I will burn everything you love.

FOR MY MEMORIETH.

TAKE

CLICK

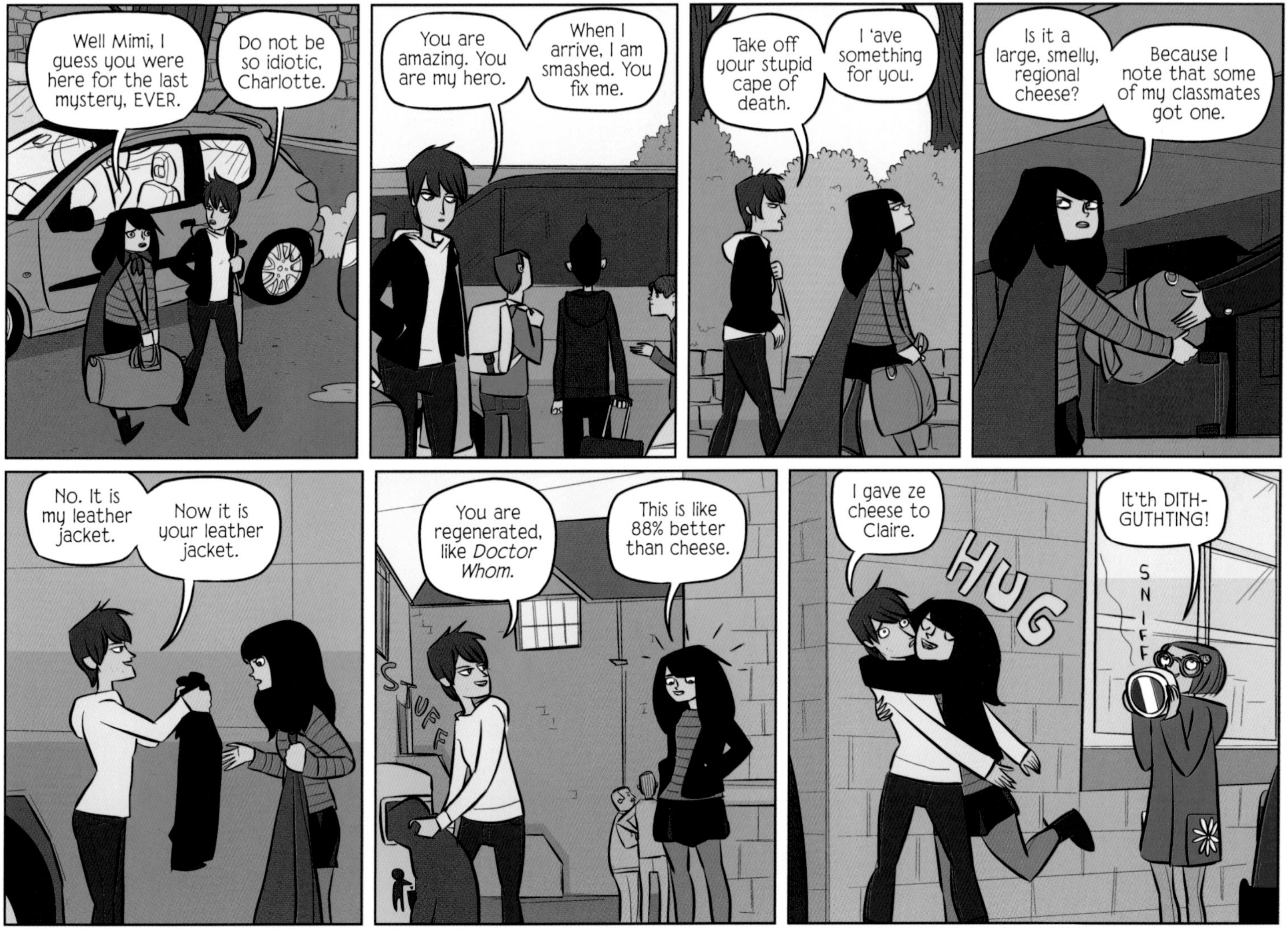
Well Mimi, I guess you were here for the last mystery, EVER.
Do not be so idiotic, Charlotte.
You are amazing. You are my hero.
When I arrive, I am smashed. You fix me.
Take off your stupid cape of death.
I 'ave something for you.
Is it a large, smelly, regional cheese?
Because I note that some of my classmates got one.
No. It is my leather jacket.
Now it is your leather jacket.
STUFF
You are regenerated, like *Doctor Whom*.
This is like 88% better than cheese.
I gave ze cheese to Claire.
HUG
It'th DITH-GUTHTING!
SNIFF

There they go. Our friends from across the water.

When will we see them again?

Next year, Lottie. March next year.

That's right, Claire. Probably never.

They don't seem scared of Camille any more.

I think that's what comes of her making a right tit of herself.

BRRUMMM

Sons Trip

Jack! Mimi said you weren't coming. But here you are.

Behind a bush.

I just wanted to see her one last time.

PLUCK

Au revoir, Jack. Au revoir Tackleford.

⟨Would you like to play Scrabble?⟩

⟨It is... *Travel Scrabble.*⟩

SCRABBLE

RATTLE

⟨Ah you are back! The saddest sister in the world!⟩

⟨Salut, Elodie.⟩

⟨Is that almost a smile?⟩

⟨I told you it would not be so bad.⟩

⟨It was not terrible. Not so very terrible.⟩

⟨Tackleford is a nice place! Weird, but nice.⟩

⟨I liked the boys there. Those Northern boys, eh? Ha ha!⟩

BOF.

⟨You kissed one of them, didn't you? I can tell!⟩

⟨It is written all over you like a newspaper!⟩

⟨NON!⟩

⟨I wrote anarchist poetry and was angry for three weeks.⟩

⟨YOU RASCAL!⟩

There Jack, a neat quiff, all it took was a bit of spit.

No more Mr Spock hair.

"STYLE"

HEY are those CIGS in your pocket?

Oh... yeah, Lauren gave me them to give to Mimi.

I'll chuck em out.

No, let's SMOKE em.

...okay...

COUGH COUGH COUGH COUGH COUGH

This was the worst idea you've EVER HAD, Charlotte Grote.

COUGH COUGH COUGH

FIN

THE END

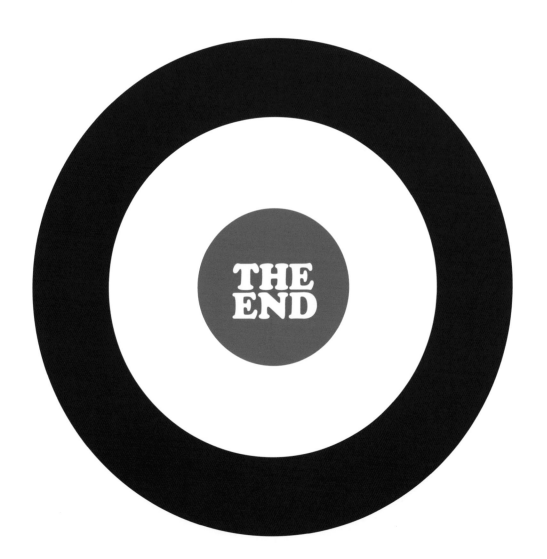

FROM THE DESK OF CHARLOTTE GROTE

Greetings, mystery enthusiast!

Thank you for reading *The Case Of The Modern Men*, a deep and meaningful glimpse into my life and the lives of several other people. I hope you enjoyed the "high octane action" which you do not get from such comic books as *Mild Funnies, Ultimate Discussion Man*, and *World Of Items*. Not to say those are not good comics. *World Of Items* features a number of fascinating pages that can used to help you get to sleep after a stressful day. And who has not enjoyed a page or two of *Mild Funnies* when on the "po"? Why, the sound of unenthusiastic laughter is the third most heard noise outside privy doors after tinkling and plops.

But it is fair to say that *TCOTMM* lacks certain familiar characters. Mildred, maybe the most beautiful and mysterious blonde phantom of Tackleford, is barely in it! And poor Mr Beckwith, who was offered entire PAGES of earlier books, barely gets chance to stick his oar in.

This is bound to be a disappointment for readers who are fond of elbow pads and emotional sensitivity. But do not fear, dear reader, because I have well got a bonus section for you.

Alongside the original feature presentation of this story, there ran a weekly feature to showcase your absent favourites. At last, collected for posterity, you can see Miss Haversham torment her dear ole Dad's colleagues. Finally—because you may have demanded it—you can enjoy the raw DANGER and dietary RISKS of Ryan and Amy's dinner eve with Mrs Lord and the predictably named "Mr Lord"! These moments, delivered in a traditional comic strip style, open the door to the humdrum world of Tackleford (hem hem) AFTER DARK!

Perhaps there are other local friends you feel did not get their turn in this book. If it is them what you are hoping for, I invite you to "go whistle", because this is what I have for you and I ain't got any more.

Kindest regards &c.

Charlotte Grote.

Boycey, have you got a girlfriend?

Er well um you know kind of?

JUSSST TELL HER HOW YOU FEEEEL

Come on Mildred, home time.

Daughter, you have to stop treating that poor man like a zoo animal.

I don't!

He's a scientist, not some beast.

Let me adopt him, Neil.

You'd let me adopt him if he was a panther.

When do you think a human being reaches true self-awareness?

I have a few ideas about this.

PAD PAD

I think it's the moment when, as a child, you don't want those inflatable Spider-Men or Disney princesses they sell on street corners any more.

CLICK

I don't know. What about grabber machines? I still want bad toys when they're in a grabber machine.

POP

PIT PIT PWUFF

The toys in grabber machines are incredibly valuable, Ryan.

That's why you can't buy them in *shops*.

Look Walt, it's your Auntie Shelley!

NO. Non Auntie. N'AUNTIE.

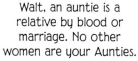

Walt, an auntie is a relative by blood or marriage. No other women are your Aunties.

You're weirdly ...*militant* about this.

Calling family friends Uncle or Auntie is more confusing than the concept that you might not be related to *everyone you know.*

I'm just drawing the line that even meddling bureacracy refuses to.

Mildred, you know you don't *have* to go to your dad's office after school any more.

But I like it there!

Wouldn't you rather just go home and play loud music until I come home?

No!

Doesn't Neil... want me at the office any more?

Of... of course he does.

Does he want me to stop teasing the science men?

You've just made this very easy.

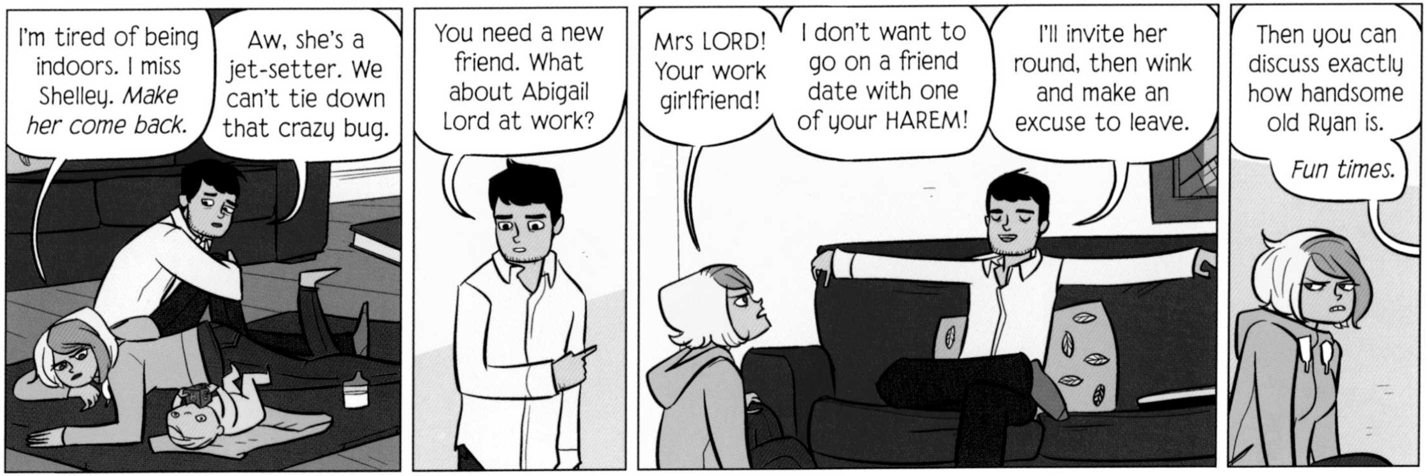
I'm tired of being indoors. I miss Shelley. *Make her come back.*
Aw, she's a jet-setter. We can't tie down that crazy bug.
You need a new friend. What about Abigail Lord at work?
Mrs LORD! Your work girlfriend!
I don't want to go on a friend date with one of your HAREM!
I'll invite her round, then wink and make an excuse to leave.
Then you can discuss exactly how handsome old Ryan is.
Fun times.

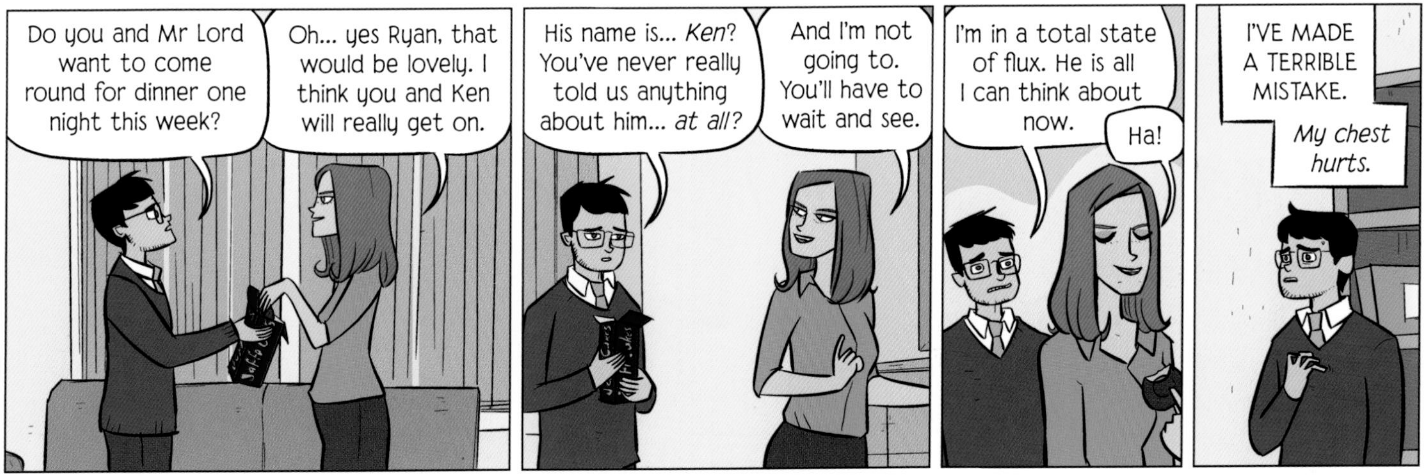
Do you and Mr Lord want to come round for dinner one night this week?
Oh... yes Ryan, that would be lovely. I think you and Ken will really get on.
His name is... *Ken*? You've never really told us anything about him... *at all*?
And I'm not going to. You'll have to wait and see.
I'm in a total state of flux. He is all I can think about now.
Ha!
I'VE MADE A TERRIBLE MISTAKE.
My chest hurts.

Bad Machinery, Volume Eight

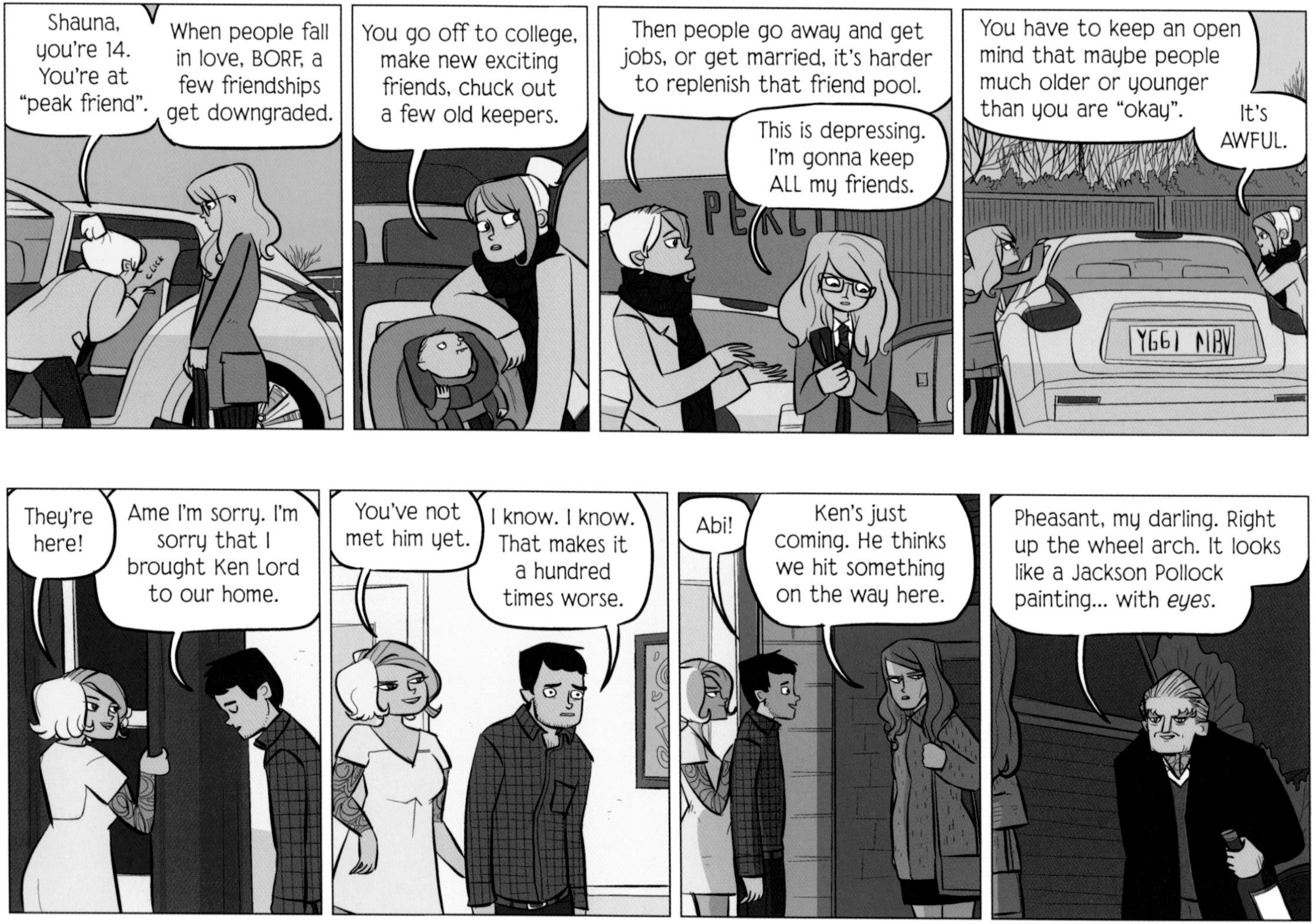
Shauna, you're 14. You're at "peak friend".
When people fall in love, BORF, a few friendships get downgraded.
You go off to college, make new exciting friends, chuck out a few old keepers.
Then people go away and get jobs, or get married, it's harder to replenish that friend pool.
This is depressing. I'm gonna keep ALL my friends.
You have to keep an open mind that maybe people much older or younger than you are "okay".
It's AWFUL.
YG61 MBV
They're here!
Ame I'm sorry. I'm sorry that I brought Ken Lord to our home.
You've not met him yet.
I know. I know. That makes it a hundred times worse.
Abi!
Ken's just coming. He thinks we hit something on the way here.
Pheasant, my darling. Right up the wheel arch. It looks like a Jackson Pollock painting... with *eyes*.

Ken is... he's... quite... *senior*... to her, isn't he?

Amy! SHH!

Oh come on, he's got to be in his late sixties. She's, what, *35*?

...I said to him, "never let them trim your sails... or your EYEBROWS"!

Stop bein' BAD!

Ryan, I spend most of my days in this house, alone, with a helpless infant.

I need this poisonous intrigue.

I need it to LIVE.

CLUTCH

You must tell me, Abi, how did you two meet?

Ken was my professor at university.

I'd read his novel, of course.

"He Caught Bass With His Hands" was my favourite book.

I was a shy little thing, but he saw something in me. Of course, we had to keep it quiet.

She puts up with me.

He's still an impressive sight, Amy. Even with his shirt off.

Are you still working on your books?

I wrote until there was nothing left to write. Then I taught.

I was a bit of a brawler in my younger days, Amy.

I know the smell of the wrestling mat. But the old fire, it dies, it goes out.

This is nice. They both made a friend.

What... *kind* of wine is this, Ryan?

Basic garage wine. If you don't like it, at least you know your insides got cleaned.

SHFF

Dad, I reckon we should get into Urban Krav Maga.

What. What?

Err, it's almost CERTAINLY the best new self defence system.

When your back's to the wall in a dive bar, you need a fighting style you can rely on.

Have you been watching Roadhouse featuring the late Mr Patrick Swayze?

I figure I'm going to make a lot of enemies in life. Got to be ready.

And, yes.